DRAG
The Strange Lega

CW00969515

Part One of
The Dragondah Mysteries

JACKIE LOXHAM

"Every now and again a book comes along that is a genuine joy to read, and I almost forget I'm meant to be critiquing it. This book certainly fell into that category for me."

ELEANOR HAWKEN Jericho Writers

"I can't wait to read Part Two. It is such a great story, for young and old. I really enjoyed the adventure. Great read!"

CHARLOTTE WALKER LoveReading4Kids

"Ottillee is instantly likeable, she is brave, determined and compassionate. Finn is a wonderful character and his friendship with Ottillee enriches the plot hugely."

KITTY WALKER Daniel Goldsmith Associates

DRAGONDAH
The Strange Legacy of Ottillee Bottomly

Part One of
The Dragondah Mysteries

JACKIE LOXHAM

HOW IT
ALL BEGAN...

I'm tired and I'm weak,

and I'll be ready to let go soon.

Life in Dragondah will carry

on without me, of course.

Birds and bats will still soar

through the ancient woodlands.

Full moons will still illuminate

the golden sands. And age-old

feuds will still simmer

away in the shadows.

Although maybe I've finally

thought of a way to let

the light back in...

'Where The Heck Is Dragondah?'

'OH, MY GIDDY AUNT!'

I winced. What was it with Mum? How often did I have to tell her that nobody in the world said 'Oh, my giddy aunt!' anymore? But she was far too busy reading her letter to even notice.

'Well, bless my soul!'

I kept my head down. If I didn't encourage Mum, she'd move on to more important things. Like me, for example. I was already perched at the kitchen table, desperate for something to eat after another hard day at Bumstead Juniors. (I'd been told off *twice*, would you believe? Once for singing too loudly in assembly and once for speaking too quietly in French.)

'You are *not* going to believe this, Ottillee!' And now Mum was waving the letter in my face. 'You've only gone and inherited some big old house in Cornwall!'

'Oh, my giddy aunt!'

I snatched the letter from her, my eyes growing wider and my heart sinking lower with every sentence I read...

TREWIN & TREMAYNE SOLICITORS

Miss Ottillee Bottomly,
c/o Mrs Grace Bottomly,
24 Church Street,
Bumstead,
London NW3   *30th April, 2018*

Dear Miss Bottomly,

We are acting on behalf of the recently deceased Mrs Cowenna Crow. You are to inherit all her worldly goods including Dragondah Hall on Cornwall's north coast. As you are still only eleven years of age, your mother will serve as your trustee until you turn eighteen. This includes a generous yearly allowance to cover your living expenses and further education.

Such a large bequest will no doubt come as a surprise to you, Miss Bottomly, especially as you never met your benefactress. But it was Mrs Crow's last wish that you were given a fresh start following your tragic loss last year. She assured us that she never missed one of Ross Bottomly's wildlife programmes, and was confident that if you'd inherited even a fraction of your father's courage, spirit and humour, her Cornish legacy would be in very good hands.

We trust that relocating to a 16th-century country house in an 'Area of Outstanding Natural Beauty' meets with your approval, Miss Bottomly, so please ask your mother to contact this office. We need to discuss the terms of the will and complete all the arrangements relating to your impending move to Dragondah.

Yours sincerely,

A. Tremayne

Arthur Tremayne Esq.

I forgot to breathe for a moment, my eyes darting between the words 'your tragic loss' and 'your impending move to Dragondah'. Everything else, the bowl of fruit on the table, the clock ticking on the wall and the red double-decker bus outside the window, faded into the background. And then, quick as a flash, my anguish turned to indignation.

'But what the heck's this woman playing at?' I met Mum's expectant gaze. 'We'd never leave Bumstead, would we? Never in a million, trillion years.'

'We wouldn't?'

'No, of course we wouldn't! I can't believe you're even *thinking* about it, Mum!'

'Well, yes, I can see it's a lot for you to take in, sweetheart.' Mum was suddenly looking shifty. 'And, of course, we'd never go to Cornwall if you were dead set against it—'

'Well, that's a relief!'

'But just think about it for a second, will you?' She sat down next to me. 'You're an heiress, Ottillee, an *heiress*. Cowenna Crow has left you all her worldly goods!'

'Huh! I'd have been much happier if she'd left me all alone!' I couldn't help retort as I scanned the letter again. 'I mean, surely this is some sort of joke? The woman only knew Dad off the telly, for heaven's sake! Didn't she have any family of her own to leave her stuff to?'

But Mum was no longer listening to me. 'Just imagine,

Ottillee, swapping the bustling streets of London for the peace and quiet of Dragondah. Breathing in the fresh sea air of one of Cornwall's beautiful sandy beaches—'

'But — but—'

'But *what*, sweetheart?' Mum's expression was dreamy, as though she was already breathing in the fresh sea air of one of Cornwall's beautiful sandy beaches.

'Where the heck *is* Dragondah? I mean, I don't even know where Cornwall is—'

'Oh, my goodness, you *don't?*' Dragged back to reality, Mum started rummaging about in her bag. Seconds later, she was showing me the brightly-coloured map she'd brought up on her tablet. 'Now, this is England, Ottillee—'

I released a heavy sigh.

'And this is London where we live right now—'

I rolled my eyes.

'—while Cornwall is a large county right down here in the southwest of England, see? It's about 250 miles away—'

'250 *miles* away!'

'Yes, Cornwall's about as far as you can go before you fall off the end of England and into the sea. And these bright green bits here—' she tapped the screen, 'are "Areas of Outstanding Natural Beauty". Oh, it's going to be so wonderful living somewhere like that.'

'Well, not for *me,* it's not. I'm going to feel like a right odd one out living in an area of outstanding natural beauty.'

I wasn't being modest here. I was pipe-cleaner skinny with limp, mousy hair that I glammed up with pigtails and a secret application of Mum's Gorgeous-Girl hair serum.

'Oh, Ottillee!' Mum chortled. 'It's the s*cenery* that's beautiful in Cornwall, not the people who live there! You'll fit in fine, honestly you will!'

Humph! I'd have taken great offence at a comment like that had I not had far more important things on my mind.

'But, Mum, you're not thinking things through properly, are you? What about your job for a kick-off?'

'Oh, Ottillee, I'm not sure I *want* to spend the rest of my life showing other people round art galleries. Your gran left me some money in her will, so I'm thinking it might be time to pick up my paintbrushes again. You know, rediscover my *own* artistic talents. I do have an art degree, you know.'

'You *do?* Golly.' But I refused to be distracted by Mum's shock disclosure for long. 'Well, what about *my* education then? It's really going to suffer if we move away from London, isn't it?'

I scowled when Mum started chortling away again. She wasn't even *trying* to take me seriously.

'Nice try, sweetheart, but you'll be leaving Bumstead Juniors in a few months anyway. And I'm sure Cornwall's secondary schools are every bit as good as London's.'

'Yeah, but what about Dylan and Ella?' My fingers crept up to my neck. 'You know they won't manage at Bumstead High without me—'

'Of course they will, Ottillee! They'll get along just fine without you. They might even be glad of the chance.' Mum's mouth twitched with amusement. 'And will you *please* leave your eczema alone?'

'Yeah, but I practically saved Dylan's life last week.' I scratched my neck even harder. 'Olivia McDonald had him in a head-lock outside Bumstead Burgers and—'

'Yes, well, I'm sure Dylan was very grateful to you, Ottillee. When he'd got over the humiliation, that is. But it's high time that boy learned to stand on his own two feet—'

'And then there's Guides, Mum. Those girls can't even put up a tent without me.'

'Oh, Ottillee, really!' Mum dragged my hand away from my neck. 'The 2nd West Bumstead Girl Guide troop will *also* get along fine without you.'

'Yeah, but next door won't, will she?' I was getting really desperate now. 'Mrs Gupta is *always* telling me I'm her only visitor under eighty — well, apart from her daughter, that is. And anyway, she's going to think I'm really ungrateful if I up and leave after she's just spent hundreds of pounds on my bezzie trainers—'

'Oh, Ottillee, I've already told you. Gold sequins might *look* very snazzy, but they cost next to nothing.' As always, Mum had an answer for everything. 'And anyway, Mrs Gupta and her daughter are welcome to visit us any time they like. Just like all our friends and neighbours. Cornwall's a really lovely part of the world and—'

But I'd stopped listening now. I didn't want to hear how lovely Cornwall was. And I *certainly* didn't want to hear how everyone could get along fine without me. I wanted to rip that solicitor's letter into tiny pieces. And I wanted to know how Mum could ever leave this cosy little 3-bedroom house we'd always shared with Dad. I lowered my eyes, the tablecloth now little more than a blur of red and green.

'Oh, Ottillee, don't get upset.' Mum sat down and hugged me to her tightly. 'I know what's *really* troubling you.'

'No, you don't,' I snivelled into her long, dark hair.

'I do, sweetheart.'

'No, you don't.'

'I do, Ottillee.'

'No, you *don't*.'

'Yes, I do, Ottillee. You're thinking about your dad, aren't you?'

Oh, why was Mum always right? She drew away from me now and met my watery gaze.

'And believe me, Ottillee, your dad would only want what's best for us. I mean, it's not like we've got any other relatives keeping us in London, is it? Or anywhere else, come to that. I think Mrs Crow was right. A fresh start is exactly what you and I need.'

'Yes, but if we move 250 miles away to Cornwall,' I blubbed, 'how the heck's Dad ever going to find us again?'

My tears were flowing freely now, and Mum's face crumpled too.

'Oh, sweetheart, I thought you'd stopped hoping for miracles like that to happen ages ago.' She wiped my face with gentle fingers. 'You seem to be getting on so much better nowadays. But if you think a few more counselling sessions would help, I'd be happy to get back in touch with Miss Roberts—'

'Oh, no, Mum, I'm fine.' I brushed her hand away impatiently. 'I was just being stupid, that's all. I know — I know Dad's never coming back to us.'

I managed a weepy smile. Because the last thing I

needed was another hour discussing my problems with Miss Roberts. And anyway, I'd found a much better way of dealing with my 'overwhelming grief' than anything she'd ever come up with.

I was secretly writing to Dad as though he was still alive. As though he hadn't been swept down the Amazon River eighteen months ago. As though he hadn't got a memorial stone in a leafy corner of Bumstead Heath. And as though it was only a matter of time before he came strolling through the front door demanding a cuppa, the latest Bumstead Rovers footie scores and one of his really annoying group hugs.

My dad is — sorry, *was* the best wildlife documentary maker on the planet. His programme *Wilderness World* won so many awards it was embarrassing. He even went to Buckingham Palace once.

Yet despite Dad's success, he never stopped pushing himself, travelling to the world's most dangerous places to film its rarest creatures. I mean, people like the royal family and this Cowenna Crow woman wouldn't even know vomiting vipers and tufted tarantulas *existed* if it weren't for Ross Bottomly. And Dad would still be taking risks like that if he hadn't taken one risk too many and—

Mum's voice suddenly broke through my thoughts. 'Anyway, Ottillee, it's probably best if I just *call* the solicitor tomorrow and get a few more details about Mrs Crow's will, okay?' She gave me a comforting pat before getting to her feet. 'And please don't worry. I'm not going to force you to move to Cornwall if you *really* don't want to, am I? Now, pasta with mushroom sauce do you for supper?'

I managed a nod despite having lost my appetite. Because I wasn't stupid, was I? I mean, as much as Mum was *saying* all the right things, I knew from the smile playing on her lips that she was going to force me to move to Cornwall. She was even humming a merry little tune as she darted about the kitchen.

Except it *wasn't* a merry little tune, was it? It was the *Wilderness World* theme tune, and before I could stop them, my eyes darted across the kitchen to Dad's Bumstead Rovers mug. Yes, there it was, still hanging on its own little hook on the dresser. Still waiting to be picked up by him any day now. Exactly like I myself had for the longest while.

And over the next few weeks, I started hoping for other miracles to happen. That Mrs Crow's relatives would claim Dragondah Hall for themselves. That Mrs Crow's solicitor had got me muddled up with some other Ottillee Bottomly who'd just lost her dad in the South American jungle. That there would be a health scare about the surprisingly harmful effects of fresh sea air on the complexions of 35-year-old mothers. Or even that this Dragondah place no longer existed. (Not as unlikely as it sounded as there was nothing about it online, and even made-up places like Camelot and Sylvania and the Scilly Isles are all over the internet nowadays, aren't they?)

But much to my dismay, it turned out Dragondah *did* exist, the relatives *didn't* exist, the solicitor *hadn't* got me mixed up, and there were *no* health scares for 35-year-old mothers. (Not about fresh sea air anyway).

Consequently, Mum returned from her sneaky solo visit to Cornwall with great affection for 'doddery old Mr Tremayne', as well as rave reviews of both Dragondah and Dragondah Hall. Oh yes, and she had a particularly determined glint in her eye too.

She soon sold 24 Church Street (as well as our squishy corner sofa, our lovely pine furniture and our deep-fat fryer) to a teacher who promised to pop in on Mrs Gupta every single week. Next, she organised a leaving party for everyone we knew, including a reassuringly tearful Ella and an upsettingly cheerful Dylan. And finally, she took me to Bumstead Heath to plant flowers on Dad's memorial stone, flowers the Bumstead Garden Centre said could pretty much look after themselves.

Then on the first Monday in August, two weeks after I'd broken up from Bumstead Juniors for the very last time,

Mum and I shut the door on our house, also for the very last time. Seven hours, four toilet stops, three ice creams and six arguments later, we were following our removal van along the winding, weed-choked driveway of our new home. My heart sank when I finally stepped out of the Mini.

Dragondah Hall was even worse in real life than it had been in my head, as tall as it was wide, and a hodge-podge of crooked roofs, shadowy porches, crumbling walls and peeling paint. Much of it was overrun with creeping ivy, the front door looked like it had turned away far more visitors than it had welcomed, and the windows were so dark and dingy that you could only guess at the secrets on the other side. Four stone crows ('gargoyles', Mum called them) were giving me the evil eye from their perches on the roof.

But what didn't bother to give me a second look was the *living* crow tearing the flesh off the dead squirrel on the front steps. Dithering doodahs! And what the heck was that skinny, grey thing racing off into those trees as though it didn't have a second to lose?

<figure>
—◦◇◦—
</figure>

2

Dad's Secret Report

DATE: Tuesday, 7 August, 2018   TIME: 6:30am

PLACE: Bedroom at Dragondah Hall   SUBJECT: Life's in ruins

Dear Dad,

I know I've not been in Dragondah a day yet, but everything's already looking bleak. Very bleak indeed. In fact, my life's in ruins.*

1) Let's get Dragondah Hall over with first. Some people (Mum) say a house can't have enough character, but I say it most definitely <u>can</u>. This one was built about a million years ago (the year 1590 is carved above the door), and I'm really hoping it doesn't last too much longer. I mean, all these rafters, beams and floorboards might <u>look</u> pretty solid, but they've <u>got</u> to be riddled with woodworm **. And you can forget all about the modern stuff we had back home in Bumstead. Can you believe we've got to wash our dishes BY HAND? And have BATHS instead of showers? And pull stupid CHAINS to flush the loos?!!! There are also some ugly gargoyles on the roof and lots of horrid brown furniture that some people (Mum again) call 'antique', but I call 'junk'.

2) And, of course, we've totally lost contact with the outside world here.*** I'm just going to have to write letters to everyone back home, aren't I? I mean, we've got no phone, no internet and no mobile signal, if that's even possible in the 21st century?!! But HUMUNGOUS NEWS, we've got no telly either. (Not even an aerial for one.) So this means Mrs Crow LIED about never missing one of your wildlife programmes, Dad. Either that or she was so old (a centenarian**** would you believe?) that she'd gone a bit — well, doolally towards the end of her life. Not that <u>Mum</u> gives two hoots we're here under false pretences. No, she's just happy to get out of London with her fancy art degree and her swanky new paintbrushes. I mean, she didn't even have the decency to pass her artistic talent on to me!!

3) Mum didn't bother telling me about Mrs Crow's stupid 'dying wishes' either. Would you believe I've got to sleep in what's pretty much the roof? Even though any of the ten <u>proper</u> bedrooms would have been okay for me. ('Calico' has got a canopy bed, for example. And 'Nutmeg' has a handy little sink.) But no, it's all the way up in the attic for me. Of course, Mum has nabbed herself a nice big room called 'Moonshine' which has a carved fireplace and a distant view of the sea. I mean, my poky old room isn't just name-less and fireplace-less and view-less, but it's also a 15-minute hike to the kitchen/fridge/biscuits. None of my London stuff looks good up here either. Not my Bumstead Rovers duvet cover. Not my stuffed animal collection. Not even your photo on my bedside table. (It's the purple frame rather than your face, Dad.) And as for my posters, Mum said she'd stuck them on my walls to 'make me feel more at home'. Well, <u>that</u> didn't work, did it?

4) Yet that's not the worst of it, Dad. Mrs Crow <u>also</u> insisted I go to some private girls' school in September. It's so far away from here that I've got to board during the week. AAAAAARGH! Anyway, all of this has only confirmed my suspicions. That Mrs Crow <u>had</u> totally lost the plot. And that my mother is getting shiftier by the minute.

5) As for Dragondah itself, what the heck am I going to do in such a boring place for the next FOUR WEEKS? And all by myself? I mean, the nearest village (Chuggypig) is a good 20 minutes' drive away. The nearest supermarket is — well, I don't think there <u>are</u> any supermarkets in Cornwall because we had to bring a whole load of stuff in the removal van. (Coffee/wine/balsamic vinegar/stinky cheeses/jars of pesto/tins of chickpeas/Mum's special face cream/Mum's special hair stuff/Mum's new painting stuff.) And it's not even outstandingly naturally beautiful here. Certainly not beautiful enough to make up for the total lack of supermarkets, cinemas, zoos, aquariums, girl guides, natural history museums, places to go for a babyccino, and nice neighbours. I don't even think there are any other <u>people</u> living here!

6) There are far too many spiders though, and I'm taking my own sweet time removing them. (Serves Mum right.) There's also a gang of evil crows skulking in the trees. One of them pooped on the Mini first chance it got. Probably the same one that's been making a racket outside my window since six this morning, despite someone (me!) throwing a sock at it. Oh, how I miss London's pigeons. At least they totally ignore you. And don't eat fluffy woodland creatures on your doorstep.

7) Mum's lost my bezzie trainers, so I can't go outside even if I wanted to. Which, of course, I don't.

8) I only have Mum to talk to, which is a pity as I'm not talking to her.

Anyway, Dad, thanks so much for listening, and a big kiss on your photo. Oh yes, and I do hope you like the rambling rose we planted on your memorial stone just before we left. And those blue flowers are forget-me-nots, by the way.

Over and out, and thinking of you as always.
Your daughter, Ottillee
xoxoxo

* The only good thing about coming to Dragondah is that Mum's promised to get me a dog.

** The woodworm is <u>sure</u> to make my eczema flare up again, probably all over my body this time.

*** Thank heavens for the radio or we wouldn't even know what day it is.

**** I'm just double-checking that you know centenarians are not soldiers in the Roman army (centurions) or people born in November and December (Sagittarians). They're people who live to be one hundred years old. Who knew, hey?!!

'A Healthy Morning Nature Walk?'

'HEY, OTTILLEE, it's a really lovely day out there. Why don't you go on a healthy morning nature walk after you've had your brekkie?'

'A healthy morning *nature* walk?' I glared at Mum over the top of my Nutty Granola. I was so mad at her for dragging me to this hellhole that I totally forgot I wasn't talking to her. 'But that's the last thing I feel like doing, Mum. And anyway, you never let me go on walks by myself. What about 'Stranger Danger' and all that kind of stuff?'

'Oh, you don't have to worry about things like that anymore, sweetheart.' She smiled at me and began gathering up the breakfast dishes. 'It's perfectly safe round these parts. Provided you don't stray *too* far, of course.'

I thought fast, taken aback by Mum's newly relaxed attitude. 'Yeah, but you know I can't find my bezzie trainers—'

'Oh, you don't have to worry about things like that

either, Ottillee.' Another serene smile as Mum got to her feet. 'Dragondah's not at all fashion-conscious.'

I released a heavy sigh of frustration. Honestly, even 250 miles away from home (and anything remotely familiar), Mum *still* thought she knew everything. I slammed down my spoon and folded my arms across my chest.

'Okay then, Mum, it's obvious you're not bothered about my happiness one little bit. So, I'll tell you what I'm going to do this morning.'

Mum started counting to herself, her gaze on the ceiling.

'One, two, three—'

'Yeah, I'll tell you *exactly* what I'm going to do.'

'Four, five, six, seven—'

'I'm going to die of boredom. That's what I'm going to do!'

'Eight, nine, TEN!'

Mum sprinted into the hallway and, by the sound of it (Bang! Thud! 'Ouch!'), launched herself into one of the packing crates. One whole minute later, and just as I was about to check she hadn't knocked herself out, my bezzie trainers came sailing through the doorway, their gold sequins flying off in all directions. Mum reappeared immediately afterwards.

'Right, Ottillee, your bezzie trainers are no longer lost!' she announced triumphantly, totally unaware of the long strip of duct tape dangling off her ponytail. 'So please put them on and go outside.'

'But Mum—'

'No, "but Mums", young lady. I'm not listening to you. It's nice and sunny out there, and the fresh sea air will do you the world of good.'

'But—'

'No, not another word, Ottillee! Because now you're getting on my last nerve too.' Mum glared at me, only to release a heavy sigh of her own. 'No, don't look at me like that, sweetheart. I've got so much to do, that's all. Unpack the crates, stock up the pantry, and then make a start on the living room. So just give me, what? Three hours or so—'

'Three hours!'

'Yes, have you seen the dust in this place? I don't know what that caretaker used to do with his days, honestly I don't.' Mum smiled at me. 'And I promise to have your favourite lunch waiting for you when you get back — you know, to celebrate our first *proper* meal together at Dragondah Hall. Now, how's that for not caring about your happiness, hey?'

Realising I was beaten, I put my bezzie trainers on my feet and my red baseball cap on my head. Then, making sure Mum knew I was doing her a massive favour, I pushed open the back door and slammed it so hard behind me that the glass shook. But thankfully didn't fall out.

'I am not going to like it out here. I am *not* going to like it out here,' I vowed as I glanced about the sunlit garden through narrowed eyes. 'And even if I *do* like it out here, I am *not* going to tell my mum.'

Because I could already tell this wasn't the worst garden I'd ever seen in my life. In fact, it was like *no* garden I'd ever seen in my life, certainly not in Bumstead. No trimmed hedges, clipped lawns or neat rows of pansies for Dragondah. No, here it was all soaring palms and exotic shrubs and giant tropical plants with leaves as large as open umbrellas. (Who knew Cornwall was quite so close to the equator?) There was no smell of traffic fumes out here either, just the scent of all sorts of wildflowers. And how peaceful everywhere was after London. I couldn't hear any beeping horns or screeching brakes or neighbours rowing over the wheelie bins anyway. All I could hear were bees buzzing, birds tweeting and—

'CAW! CAW! CROOOOAK!'

Aaagh! I'd forgotten about the gang of evil crows. A particularly big one, its black feathers speckled with white, was glaring down at me from the roof. It was probably mad that our Mini was now out of its pooping range in the garage.

'CAW! CAW! CROOOOOOOOAK!'

the crow went again and this time, I'd had enough.

'Shut your beak, you Cornish birdbrain, you!' I shouted, throwing in a fist shake for good measure. 'Poop on me if you think you're hard enough!'

The bird flew off in a huff, and I congratulated myself on a job well done. Of course, I knew I shouldn't have been so childish or insulting to Cornish people, but sometimes you have to let your frustrations out, don't you? On someone other than your mother. She was currently peering at me through the window with a concerned expression on her face, and I waved her away with what I hoped was a reassuring smile. Then I turned my cap around (just in case the 'Cornish birdbrain' was out for revenge) and set off along the path.

And it turned out the crow wasn't the only creature rattled by my unexpected appearance in the garden. Sparrows scattered, blackbirds bolted and a squirrel threw itself into the flower borders. But soon, I'd reached the lawn and was meandering past a pond with beautiful lilies and darting dragonflies, not to mention a statue of a nuddy nymph. (Ooops, no, my mistake, it was a nuddy discus-thrower, tee-hee.) Then it was on to an orchard, its trees heavy with apples and the biggest cherries I'd ever seen in my life. (Ooops, no, my mistake, they were the smallest plums.)

A high stone wall was waiting for me through the fruit trees, and I eyed its arched wooden gate with the lowest of expectations. I mean, why I was even bothering to wander over and struggle with its rusty latch, I didn't know. There was hardly likely to be a bustling high street with a wide choice of child-friendly shops, pizzerias and cinemas on

the other side of it, was there? No, I told myself as the latch finally gave way, the most I could hope for was a boring old field or a boring old lane or a boring old — golly, it was a boring old *wood!*

And the wood wasn't boring at all, my eyes wide as I stepped into its cool shadows and glanced about me. The path I was standing on was so overgrown with brambles and ferns that I doubted anyone had used it in years. The trees that were towering above me were all wrinkled with age, their bulging roots covered with moss, and their leafy branches blocking the blue summer sky from my gaze. Neither a chirp nor a rustle could be heard in the undergrowth. And then all of a sudden, a bright ray of sunlight pierced the ancient woodland canopy, and the next few seconds were all a bit of a blur.

'EEEEEEEK!'

No sooner had I reopened my eyes than the last thing I'd ever expected to see had come soaring out of the trees straight towards me. A bat! But not one of those tiny bats that used to swoop about Bumstead Heath after dusk. Bats so fast and fleeting you could almost have imagined them. No, this bat was impossible to miss, and not just because it was broad daylight. Its leathery wings were stretched out either side of a body that was easily as big as a rat's. Its mouth was wide open to reveal two scary-looking fangs.

'EEEEEEEEEEEK!'

I shot back through the gate so fast that my baseball cap flew off, most likely never to be seen again. But to my dismay, not to mention the noisy delight of the lurking crow, the bat seemed to regard my dash for cover as a game. It flew after me into the garden, darting about the lawn like a demented wasp on the lookout for an open window. The creature then did a couple of showy loop-the-loops so close to my head that I fell to the ground. But before I could recover my dignity, the bat had flown off, and the crow had stopped making a racket. Peace and quiet had returned to the garden. But not for long.

'Come back here, you little wretch, you!' A voice rang out through the orchard. Then whoever was there uttered a very rude word beginning with 's'. Then a slightly rude word beginning with 't'. Then two words that weren't rude at all and began with 'b's.

'Blithering barnacles!'

I struggled to my feet to see a boy emerging from the leafy cover of the fruit trees. He looked about my age and was wearing a red baseball cap. *My* red baseball cap, if I wasn't very much mistaken.

'Hey, you!' I yelled, so indignant that I forgot all about

my run-in with the hooligan bat. 'That's *my* cap, that is!'

'You don't say?' Clearly astonished to see me, the boy came to an abrupt halt. But he recovered quickly enough, brazenly twisting the cap round to the back of his head before meeting my gaze full on. 'I found the little beauty in some brambles just now. Thought some piskies had left it for me, I did.'

'Well, you thought wrong. Because *I* left it for you and—'

'That's very kind of you, thank—'

'No, I didn't leave it for you *deliberately*. I left it for you by mistake.'

'Oh well, finders keepers, losers weepers, that's what my old nan always likes to say.'

'Yeah, well, my old *mum* always likes to say—'

But Mum rarely said anything deep and meaningful, my humiliation complete when the — the *cap burglar* wedged my hat cvcn further down on his head. Huh! Talk about cocky! I mean, all I needed now was for Mum to dash out of the house and tell me off for calling her 'old'. And the newcomer to wrestle me to the ground and stuff a dandelion up my nose — which was what the older boys at Bumstead High liked to do given half a chance.

But no, nothing like that happened. There was no dashing or telling off from Mum, and all the boy did was trudge across the grass towards me. As he got closer, I couldn't help notice how skinny he was. Quite scruffy too if I'm honest. His T-shirt looked like it had been through the wash a hundred times, his baggy jeans were held up by a cord, and his trainers — well, the less said about those, the better.

'*A-blah-blah-blah-wek?*' the boy asked as he came to a halt about ten steps away from me. But I didn't respond, and not just because I didn't understand what he'd said. No, I'd found myself distracted by his pale skin and the way his jet-black hair grew long on his neck. And then there was his wide mouth and the cleft in his chin, as deep as if someone had dug it out with a chisel.

'*A-blah-blah-kewsel-kerne-wek?*' the boy repeated patiently if quite a bit louder.

'What — what does that mean?' I stuttered, my fingers reaching for my neck. Although why I was so nervous, I didn't know. Mum had told me the people down here might speak in some 'ancient and noble language' of their own. I just hadn't expected them to do it so soon. Or in my own back garden.

'Just asking if you spoke Cornish, that's all.' Even the boy's English sounded strange to my ears, to tell you the truth.

'No, I'm sorry, I don't,' I replied, not sure why I was apologising either. I mean, ancient and noble languages hadn't even been on the curriculum at Bumstead Juniors. (Most of us had enough trouble with French.)

'Mmmm, well, that's a great pity, I must say,' the boy replied with a straight face, but I wasn't stupid, was I? I knew he was mimicking — or rather *exaggerating* my way of talking now, making me sound like I had a plum in my mouth. But my scowl went unnoticed as he was now looking about the garden. After a few awkward seconds, I felt it was up to me to fill the silence.

'So what's your name then?' I asked, doing my best to put the teasing and the stolen baseball cap to the back of my mind. 'My name's Ottillee Rose Violet Bottomly and I'm eleven years old — well, eleven and three-quarters, if you really want to know.'

'Oh, Ottillee Rose Violet Bottomly, is it?' The boy's sudden smile was so wide that it lit up his face. His eyes narrowed, his chin formed a point, and a spurt of laughter looked like it might burst out of his mouth at any second. Then he stepped forward and reached out his hand towards me.

'Nice to meet you,' was all he said. 'I'm Finn.'

Was I just imagining it, or did the speckled crow croak approvingly in the trees?

———∞◇◇∞———

4

'A Flittermouse?'

I FELT AWKWARD as I took Finn's hand in mine. I wasn't a big fan of shaking hands, to tell you the truth. It reminded me of Dad's memorial service back in London when I'd shaken hands with everyone from the vicar to Dad's boss, Sir Michael Rabbit-Burrows. (At one point I'd even shaken hands with Mum when all she'd wanted to do was pass me another tissue.) But then I looked directly into Finn's eyes and stifled a gasp. Because the eyes that were looking back at me were really strange yet also strangely familiar. *And that was because one of them was blue and the other one was green.*

I mean, what were the chances of that, hey? And for a few heart-stopping seconds, I could feel Dad's warm hugs and scratchy kisses as he teased me over something or other. Usually my wonky fairy cakes. Or my reluctance to pick up a slug. Or my inability to take a penalty under pressure.

'Finn what?' I asked, slightly less stiffly.

'Just Finn,' Finn replied casually, as though surnames and middle names were just for girls. He considered me for a long moment. 'So where did you get a name like Ottillee from anyway?'

I scowled. 'From my parents, of course.'

'No, I mean, where did *they* get it from? I've never heard it before.'

Now it was my turn to consider Finn for a long moment. I was debating whether to tell him the lie I always told whenever I knew my mum couldn't hear me. The one about my glamorous granny Ottillee whose husband had thrown her off a round-the-world cruise when he'd caught her playing Monopoly with the captain. But then I looked into Finn's blue-green eyes and decided — well, to sidestep the question entirely. (I mean, Finn had probably never even *heard* of the Sylvanian Families anyway.)

'Haven't a clue where they got the name Ottillee from,' I fibbed in a tone that invited no further enquiry. Because I had a few questions of my own now.

'So, how old are *you* then, Finn?'

"Oh, that's a tricky one.' He shrugged. 'Eleven too, I suppose.'

'You *suppose?*'

'Yeah, give or take a few years.'

'But haven't your mum and dad told you?'

'Never spoken to them in my life.'

'You *haven't?*' My eyes widened. 'But why not?'

'Because both of them are deaders, I'm thinking.'

'You're *thinking?*' My eyes widened even further. 'You mean you're not sure your parents are *dead?*'

'I'm not sure, no. No one's ever mentioned them to me, but I suppose they *must* be dead. Otherwise, they'd have dropped by, don't you think? To check I was brushing my teeth. And eating my tatties.'

'Your tatties?'

'Yeah – my, erm, my potatoes.'

'Oh, right, yeah,' I muttered, hardly able to believe my ears. Not only was Finn a cap burglar with eyes like my dad's, but he was also an orphan. And even more astonishing, being an orphan didn't seem to bother him one bit. I mean, I was only *half* an orphan and it bothered me more than anything else in the world. Especially since I had no other living family members to my name. (Other than Mum who was always there, so didn't really count, of course.)

'Who looks after you then?' I asked, my eyes darting over Finn's ill-fitting clothes in sudden concern. 'I hope you don't mind me saying this, but you're a bit — well, skinny, aren't you?'

'Oh, skinny, is it? You're a fine one to talk — look here!'

And with this, Finn pulled up his left sleeve and flexed his arm muscles. I must confess I was mightily impressed, although I'd rather die than admit it. The boy was far too pleased with himself as it was.

'Yep, Ottillee, you've no need to worry about *me* not eating properly. Nanna Nessa's the best cook in the whole of Cornwall, she is.'

'Oh, good.' I was pleased we were finally getting somewhere. 'So Nanna Nessa's your gran, is she?'

'Suppose she must be.' Another careless shrug. 'The only thing I know for certain is that Nan looks after me a treat and has done my whole life. Three meals a day and four on Sundays.'

'Well, that's a relief, anyway.' I smiled at him. 'I mean, who wants to rely on yucky school dinners every day, hey?'

But Finn was literally bursting with pride now. 'Oh, I wouldn't know the first thing about school dinners,' he said happily. 'Never been to school in my life, I haven't. Nanna Nessa teaches me all the stuff I need to know.'

Crikey! Another bombshell. I hadn't even realised *not* going to school was an option down here in Cornwall. Although at least it was comforting to know that if my new boarding school didn't work out, my mother could take over my education. (That would serve her right for stopping me from going to Bumstead High with my friends, wouldn't it?) Then suddenly I realised Finn was asking me a question. Basically, why the heck was I wandering about Dragondah Hall's grounds like I owned the place?

'Well, that's because I *do* own the place, I suppose!'

'You're kidding?'

'Nope. Mum and I moved in yesterday.'

'Crikey!' He looked astonished. 'Your dad too?'

'No, my dad's, erm, well, he's missing.'

'Missing? Missing where?'

'Sorry, sorry,' I shook my head as if I was trying to fix some faulty wiring deep inside my brain. 'What I *meant* to say was my dad's, erm, he's, erm—'

'He's *what*?'

'Well, he's dead. Almost two years it's been now.'

No one was more shocked than me when I said the 'd' word out loud. There was no coming back from a word like that, and I'd certainly never said it before. I was just trying to act — well, *cool* like Finn, I suppose. After all, he'd lost both his parents, not just one of them. But, knowing I couldn't act cool for much longer, I didn't give Finn the chance to quiz me anymore. Instead, I launched into the whole sorry saga that was my unexpected, not to mention unwanted, inheritance.

'Blithering barnacles, Ottillee! Some people are never happy!' Finn exclaimed when I'd finished going on about the woodworm and the toilet chains and the non-existent mobile signal and how Cowenna Crow had made it up about watching my dad on the telly. 'Don't worry *why* Mrs Crow left you all her worldly goods. Just be thankful she did!'

'Thankful?' I scowled at the house over my shoulder. The gargoyles were still glowering at me from their rooftop perches, and I certainly didn't *feel* very thankful.

'Of course. You're the new Mistress of Dragondah Hall, you are!'

'Yeah, I suppose I am,' I muttered, rather taken aback by my new title. Rather taken aback by how much I *liked* it, to tell you the truth. Suddenly, I was no longer Miss Ottillee Bottomly from Bumstead. I was *Mistress* Ottillee Bottomly from Dragondah. The sort of person who enjoyed long lie-ins. Who wore twinset cardies. Who ate cucumber sandwiches. Who had beautiful dragonflies dancing about her lily pond. And who might even employ an elderly butler one day. An elderly butler called Chivers who liked to look down his nose at all her visitors—

'Although I always felt sorry for Mrs Crow, of course.' Finn's words interrupted my increasingly lofty thoughts. 'A poor old lady living somewhere so big all by herself. I often used to see her peering out of an upstairs window. She always looked really unhappy to me. Never even banged on the glass when I scrumped her apples.'

'What? You actually *knew* Mrs Crow?' My eyes were wide. 'But what was she like, Finn? Had she gone a bit, you know, *dotty?* And did she have any relatives who might want to live in Dragondah Hall, do you know? Because I'd hate to offend anyone, and me and Mum, well, we could easily move back to Bumstead—'

'Oh, no, Ottillee, I didn't know Mrs Crow at all. Truth is, no one knew her. She was a recluse, you see.'

'A recluse?' My eyes widened even further. I knew exactly what a recluse was. Someone who shut themselves off from the world. Like hermits. And lighthouse keepers. And Dylan after one of our arm-wrestling competitions.

'Yeah, I did ask my nan about Mrs Crow once, but she didn't seem to know very much. Although—'

'Although what?'

'She did say something that stuck in my head, strangely enough. Something about "giddy teenage girls", I think. Oh, yeah, and then she said something about "people making their beds and lying on them". And then she clammed up, and I've never liked to mention the old lady again.'

I nodded, mulling over Finn's words. Suddenly my benefactress was no longer some faceless old centenarian whose death had pretty much ruined my life. No, she was a person in her own right with — well, it sounded like quite an intriguing past. I mean, what had happened to change Mrs Crow from a giddy Cornish teenager into an unhappy Cornish recluse? Did she have a terrible falling out with her family, I wondered?

'Do you think I could speak to your nan about Mrs Crow?' I asked. 'She might open up a bit more to me. She might even have some idea why the old lady left me her house.'

'Yeah, sure, you can, Ottillee.' Finn shrugged as though the matter was of little importance to him. 'You'll find us if you follow the trail through the woods and turn right along the sea path. We're just across from Dragondah Island—'

'Dragondah *Island?*'

'Yeah, and Dragondah Castle.'

'Dragondah *Castle?*'

This was the first I was hearing about any islands or castles. But Finn was no longer listening to me, his eyes scanning the garden instead.

'What are we looking for?' I asked as I followed his gaze.

'Well, I don't know what *you're* looking for, Ottillee, but I'm looking for my flittermouse. Don't suppose you've seen the little feller hereabouts, have you? I'm sure I spotted him heading this way.'

'A flittermouse?' I frowned down at the grass, only for Finn to chuckle.

'Oh, a flittermouse won't give you any trouble, Ottillee. A flittermouse is far too busy zooming about the place to bother girls. You know, zapping dragonflies before they know what's hit them. Zap! Zap! Zap!' Finn made some violent, insect-zapping gestures with his hands. 'A flittermouse is as fast as lightning, he is. And he's got these ginormous fangs. Gnash! Gnash! Gnash! And—'

'Oh!' I cried as the penny finally dropped. 'You're not talking about a mouse. You're talking about a *bat!'*

'A bat, yes, of course.'

'Then why the heck didn't you say so?'

'Bat? Flittermouse? What's the difference, hey?'

Honestly, Finn was starting to get on my last nerve now. So much so that I nearly denied all knowledge of ever seeing his stupid bat. But then I gave in.

'Actually, I did see a flitter — I mean, a *bat* just now. It gave me quite a shock actually. But then it flew away, sort of up there somewhere.' I waved my hand in the air, not quite sure of Finn's intentions. 'You're not going to hurt it, are you?'

'As if I'd do that!' Finn threw me a look. 'But if he keeps on flying off during the day like this, Shadow will be the death of *me* soon enough, I don't mind admitting—'

'Shadow?' I couldn't hide my astonishment. 'You mean you've given the bat a *name?*'

'Of course, Ottillee! Shadow's lived with us forever, hasn't he?' Finn's grin said he enjoyed shocking me. 'Nan said that was the perfect name for him because he's always hanging round in the background. Clever, hey?'

'Humph!' I wasn't impressed. 'Well, Shadow certainly wasn't hanging round in the background when he saw *me*. He chased me into the garden and knocked me over!'

Finn chuckled fondly. 'Oh, I'm sure he was just playing with you.' But then his expression darkened. 'Although he hasn't got the best eyesight, I'll admit. He's a nighter, see—'

'A *nighter?*'

'Yeah, you know, he usually only goes out after dark. Flies over to the castle for a bit of a snoop around, and that's usually about it.' Finn's eyes narrowed on me. 'In fact, he probably mistook you for that tramp who's been lurking about Dragondah these past few months. A right nasty piece of work *he* looks with his coat, and his hair, and his dodging out of the way the second he sets eyes on you—'

'But Mum said it was perfectly safe round here—'

'CAW! CAW! CROOOOAK!'

Suddenly I was interrupted by what sounded like a warning cry from the crow. And that's exactly what it was. The silvery grey animal that I'd spotted racing off into the trees just after we arrived yesterday was slinking across the grass towards us.

I cautioned Finn not to make any sudden moves, only to ignore my own advice when the creature threw back its head and let loose a series of high-pitched cries. We were clearly trespassing on its territory, and I grabbed hold of Finn to drag him away, only for him to shake me off with a chuckle.

'Oh, don't worry yourself, Ottillee,' he said. 'That's just my Vixen, that is.'

'*Vixen?* You mean that's a *fox?* But she's totally the wrong colour for a fox—'

'Oh, no, she isn't, Ottillee! Vixen's just a very special fox, that's all. In fact, she's the only silver fox in all of Cornwall! Why don't you come and say hello to her?'

Finn's voice was bubbling with laughter now, much to my annoyance. Honestly, first a giant bat called Shadow and now a silver fox called Vixen. I mean, what other weird pets did this boy have? A monster slug called Samson snoring away in his underpants? A blonde hedgehog called Henrietta crouched beneath his — no, *my* red baseball cap?

I kept a wary eye on the fox as I followed Finn down the lawn. Vixen was sizing me up equally carefully, her black-tipped ears pricked, and her golden eyes bright with — well, I was hoping for intelligence rather than hostility. And then, just as I was building myself up to stroke her silver fur, she startled me by giving a series of short, sharp barks. Before I knew it, she'd darted back through the orchard towards the woods.

'Come on, Ottillee!' Finn had already set off in hot pursuit. 'Shadow's in danger, he is!'

'But — but who told you that?' I cried, looking all about me. Had I missed something? Had somebody else joined us? But Finn just ran even faster.

'Vixen told me, of course,' he shouted over his shoulder. 'Now come on. Let's get after her!'

5

'Can Vixen Swim?'

MY EYES DARTED between the house and the orchard. My fingers scratched at my neck. The speckled crow cawed encouragement from the trees. Did I take a chance and run into the woods after Finn? Or did I stay in the garden, safe and secure and, erm, normal?

I mean, yes, Mum had wanted me to keep out of her hair for the next few hours, but she'd wanted me to go on a nature walk, not chase into the unknown after strange boys. Although it was only *one* strange boy, wasn't it? And it wasn't as if I had anything better to do this morning. If I returned to the house, Mum would be sure to stick a duster in my hand.

'Wait for me, Finn!' I shrieked. 'I'm coming!'

I sprinted through the gate as fast as my bezzie trainers would carry me. All I could hear was my own huffing and puffing as I did my best to keep Finn in view. But the wood's twisted roots were doing their best to trip me up, giant ferns were blocking my path, and only brief glimpses of the red baseball cap confirmed I was even on the right track. Then seconds after I'd lost not only my breath but Finn too, I bumped right into him. He was waiting for me against the trunk of a tree, not even panting to my great annoyance.

'Come on, you slowcoach!'

'*Whas — whas* the rush?' I managed to get out, far too winded to take my usual offence.

'Shadow needs our help, that's what the rush is.' Finn was already raring to go again. 'I wouldn't be surprised if that blasted tramp wasn't giving him some sort of trouble. Looks just the type, he does.'

'Oh, Finn, of *course*, the blasted tramp won't be giving him any trouble. Chance would be a fine thing!' I was still puffed out and playing for time. 'And anyway, you can't call them "blasted tramps" nowadays, you know. You've got to call them "blasted rough sleepers".'

But Finn didn't seem to care about saying the right thing. Confirmed by his next words.

'Giss on!' he cried, grabbing my hand and yanking me along behind him. 'Now, I know you're a girl and all that, but could you stop talking rubbish and try to keep up with me?'

Huh! *That* was a challenge if I'd ever heard one. How dare Finn call me 'a girl' in such a snotty way? I mean, I'd never been so insulted in my whole life.

'Course I can keep up with you!' I cried. 'I can even beat you, you loser!'

And before Finn knew it, I'd filled my lungs with air and was sprinting off through the woods. I didn't even pull the brakes on when I heard him yelling some nonsense about 'sheep dips' at me. And then suddenly the trees were no more, the sun was in my eyes, and Finn was grabbing tight hold of my wrist.

'Stop Ottillee! STOP, will you!'

'AAAAAAAARGH!'

Because a few more steps and I'd have plunged over the edge of a cliff to my sure and certain death. The shock forced my legs to buckle beneath me and the blood to drain from my face. And as I sat on the grass with my head between my knees, I was imagining my body bouncing off the rocks like a rag doll. And Mum at my funeral, racked with guilt at her own part in my untimely demise. ('Oh, my giddy aunt!' she'd say to my sobbing friends. 'How was *I* to know there was a sheer drop just minutes from our beautiful new house?')

A peek over the edge of the precipice didn't do much to calm my frazzled nerves either. Dithering doodahs! How high up we were. How the heck was I still *alive?* Yet gradually, my panic subsided, my breathing eased, and I was able to take in the sandy little cove far beneath me.

The golden beach was edged with a sea so blue and so sparkly that it almost made my eyes ache. I mean, how beautiful it all looked on this cloudless August day. How *outstandingly naturally beautiful*, you might even say. But a glance at Finn was to see his own eyes still glinting with anger. I struggled to my feet, determined to stick up for myself.

'You could have warned me, you know, Finn!'

'I *did* warn you, you skogyn!'

'No, you did not! You just kept banging on about sheep dips!'

'Not sheep dips, Ottillee! *Steep cliffs!* You could have killed yourself, you could!'

I met Finn's steady gaze for a long moment, pondering the best way to get out of this one. I mean, honestly, this know-it-all Dragondah boy was going to think I was a right cloth-eared London dimwit. And then luckily, I spotted something out of the corner of my eye.

'Well, at least I know where Vixen is!' I cried, pointing over his shoulder. A wooden stairway was zig-zagging its way down the rocky outcrop behind him, the streak of silver that was Finn's fox already at the bottom of it.

'Well, what a little scallywag, she is!' Thankfully, Finn was now directing his scowl in *Vixen's* direction. 'So she wants us to follow her all the way down to the beach, does she?'

'Yeah, as if we'd do that!' I scoffed. 'Even from here, you can see those rickety old steps aren't safe. Just goes to show you, doesn't it, Finn? Foxes aren't quite as clever as everyone says they are.'

But Finn had already set off for the steps too. Now, why had he done that? And what was I supposed to do now, left all alone on a clifftop like Billy — I mean, *Milly* No-mates?

I sneaked another look over the edge of the precipice and grimaced. Dad had always taught me safety first when it came to long drops. And anyway, Mum would never let me forget it if I didn't show up for lunch. Especially when she'd gone to all the trouble of making me my favourite macaroni cheese with a twist. But if I stayed where I was, Finn would never let me forget it either. (I mean, how dare he call me 'a girl' in such a smart-alecky *boy* way?) I made up my mind, and a few heart-pounding minutes later, I'd survived the wooden stairway, cleared the stones at the top of the beach and was joining him on the sand.

'One hundred steps exactly!' I gasped as I bent down to examine my bezzie trainers. (I was thrilled with my death-defying antics, if not the fact that most of my sequins had fallen off.) 'Although those four dodgy ones in the middle hardly count as steps at all, do they?'

But Finn's only concern was for his animals. 'I can't believe it, Ottillee! Vixen's vanished into thin air again. What the heck's up with her?'

The two of us scanned the deserted cove with worried eyes, just some darting dragonflies and scurrying birds disturbing the peaceful scene. Although the tide was clearly on its way in, the strip of golden sand getting narrower with every gentle surge of the waves.

'Can Vixen swim?' I asked, looking out at the turquoise sea and half-expecting to see her bushy silver tail powering her towards Ireland. Or Wales. Or America. (I hadn't quite got my bearings yet.)

'Nope, Vixen would rather die than get her fur wet.' Finn stroked his chin thoughtfully. 'Now, why would she lead us all the way down here if it wasn't to rescue Shadow?'

I considered my companion carefully for a moment. 'Do you think you could have — you know, got it *wrong?*' I finally ventured. 'I mean, it can't be easy understanding what a fox is trying to tell you, and—'

'Hey, look up there!' Suddenly Finn was whooping and pointing at the sky. 'Shadow *is* here! I was right all along.'

I could indeed see the bat swooping about the cove. He didn't appear to be in any trouble though, performing a showy tailspin before dive-bombing his master over and over again. Finn bent down to pick up his dislodged baseball cap before grinning at me.

'He's just showing off because you're here,' he whispered, and I did my best to look suitably honoured.

'Yeah, I *told* you that poor tramp wouldn't have anything

to do with Shadow going off, didn't I? I mean, catching bats is no easy matter, you know.'

'Yeah, I *will* admit that Shadow only comes to you when it suits him, the little scallywag.' Finn hesitated a second before whistling and patting his right shoulder. 'Nothing like a bit of encouragement though, is there? He really shouldn't be flying about like this during the day.'

But unfortunately for us, Finn's 'little scallywag' seemed quite content to circle above our heads during the day. Indeed, Shadow was throwing in complex manoeuvres whenever he could, each one bringing him closer and closer to the sheer rock face.

'Come on now!' Finn scolded after a particularly daring loop-the-loop. 'I know you're an ace flyer and all that, but your sight's not that — oh, no!'

Suddenly Finn's eyes grew wide with shock. As for me, I gasped with horror and covered my face with my hands. Because Shadow had badly misjudged his last move and flown slap-bang into the side of the cliff.

———◦◦◇◦◦———

6

'Shapeshifting?'

FINN RACED TOWARDS the cliffs. I followed at a slower pace, bracing myself for what I was sure I was going to find. A sobbing boy and a squashed bat. But as I clambered across the stones towards him, Finn wasn't crying into Shadow's mangled little body as I feared. No, he was pointing towards a boulder, his expression a mixture of relief and something that I couldn't quite put a name to yet.

'You're not going to believe what's behind this giant rock here,' he said as I approached. 'Would you believe Shadow's flown into a cave? A *secret* cave! I'll bet you my last Cornish pasty that's where Vixen's gone as well.'

I quickened my pace, not just thrilled by Shadow's survival but also that something as exciting as a secret cave could be right on my doorstep. And yes, I *could* see a narrow opening in the cliff face. I grabbed Finn's arm and pulled him towards it.

'Come on!' I cried when I felt him dig in his heels. 'Don't you want to rescue your animals?'

'Course I do, Ottillee, but this'll do the trick much better.'

Finn's whistle was as ear-splitting as it was unexpected. But not even a crab scuttled out onto the beach. Finn's second whistle got the same disappointing result, although by this time, I had other things to worry about. The waves were surging higher up the sand with every second that passed, and Dad had always drilled into me the hidden dangers of the English seaside. Hidden dangers like riptides and fast currents and high tides that cut you off while you were trying to stop pesky seagulls from stealing your ice cream. Or in this case, trying to rescue wily foxes and wayward bats from secret caves.

'Come on, Finn,' I urged. 'Let's just go in the cave and get your animals out. The water's going to be right up soon.'

'But, Ottillee, you don't understand.' Finn gripped my arm, his eyes wide in his face. 'There could be anything in that cave.'

And then I did understand. 'Oh, I get it now. You think your tramp — sorry, your *rough sleeper* might be in there, don't you? Well, I'm pretty sure you don't have to worry about him. We had a rough sleeper back home—'

'But I don't mean—'

'Yeah, Bumstead Billy couldn't have been nicer,

honestly he couldn't.' I chuckled as I remembered the whiskery old man testing me on my French vocabulary outside Bumstead Library. 'And chances are, your rough sleeper's exactly the same as ours — just some poor old teacher who's a bit down on his luck.'

Finn rolled his eyes. 'Yeah, well, he'd have to be really down on his luck if he was living in one of *our* caves, wouldn't he?'

'Why?'

'Because he'd drown every high tide, that's why.'

'Oh, yeah.' I nodded slowly. 'I never thought of that.'

'Exactly, Ottillee. You should do a bit less talking and a bit more listening sometimes. No, the only thing living in that cave is—'

Finn mumbled something, his voice so quiet that I had to ask him to repeat himself. Twice. Stupidly, I thought he'd said something about a dragon.

'I *did* say a dragon,' he finally ground out, his frustration obvious.

'Oh, my giddy aunt, Finn!' I cried with wide-eyed astonishment. 'Dragons don't actually *exist* in real life! Surely you know that by now?'

'No, Ottillee, I don't know that at all.' Finn met my gaze squarely now. 'Look what happened years ago to poor Jago Jones.'

'Jago Jones? Who's he?'

'Oh, just some bossy-boots outsider who thought he knew better than everyone else.' Finn didn't say 'exactly like you, Ottillee', but I could tell those words were on the tip of his tongue.

'Why? What *did* happen to him?' I asked, fascinated despite myself.

'Oh, the papers said he'd drowned, but Nanna Nessa wasn't fooled. She knew he'd got too close to the—' Finn made a face like a constipated monster, 'and had paid the ultimate price.'

'So you think the—' I made my own constipated monster face, '*ate* Jago Jones?'

'Well, they never found his body, did they?'

My heart lurched in my chest. Because they'd never found my dad's body either, had they? But then I blinked hard a couple of times and tried to concentrate on what Finn was saying.

'Yeah, the dragon's got no mercy, Ottillee, no mercy at all. And quite the trickster it is too, shapeshifting into—'

'*Shapeshifting?*'

'Yeah, shapeshifting into a king crab. Or maybe even a beautiful starfish—'

'You mean so it can breathe underwater?'

'No, the dragon can already do that, you skogyn.' Finn was looking at me as though *I* was the mad one. 'It shapeshifts into harmless creatures so that it can lure the kids *inside* the cave. You know, make them forget how dangerous these places really are, especially the know-it-all kids like Jago—'

'Yeah, well, *I* think you're being a bit unfair on poor old Jago.' I couldn't help sticking up for Dragondah's ill-fated visitor. 'Maybe he was just an *adventurous* sort of boy? I mean, I quite like exploring caves myself, Finn. A few years back, my dad took me and my friends Ella and Dylan inside these really spooky caves not far from London—'

'Yeah, but we're talking about *Dragondah's* caves now,' Finn interrupted impatiently. 'And it doesn't matter what sort of kids go in them, fact is they never come out again. The dragon's pounced on them before they know what's hit them.'

I looked at this strange boy for a moment, knowing I'd got to phrase my next question very carefully.

'Erm, Finn?' I ventured.

'Yeah?'

'You don't believe in the Tooth Fairy, do you?'

'Course not.'

'Or the Easter Bunny?'

'No, I do *not!* And I don't believe Father Christmas comes down the chimney either.' Finn's mouth tightened. 'And I know what you're thinking, Ottillee—'

'No, you don't—'

'Yes, I do.'

'No, you don't.'

'Course, I do! You don't think the dragon exists, do you?'

'Mmmm, well—'

'Well, nothing.' Finn's eyes were blazing. 'Honestly, you're a right one you, aren't you, Ottillee Bottomly? You've only been here five minutes, and already you're an expert on the place. How would Dragondah have got its *name* if there wasn't a dragon living here?'

'Well, erm—' My gaze shifted to the lone dragonfly dancing high above his head. 'Could it be, erm—'

'What?'

'Well, there do seem to be quite a lot of, you know, *dragonflies* round these parts—'

'*Dragonflies!*' Finn snorted. 'Honestly, Ottillee, it wasn't a dragonfly that *ate* Jago Jones, was it?'

Finn saw my hesitation and pressed home his advantage.

'Yeah, got no answer to that one, have you? And don't forget my nan's lived in Dragondah for years and years, unlike you. She knows what's what, and she'd never lie to me about *anything*. I just know she wouldn't.'

Something flickered across Finn's face. But if it was doubt, it vanished quickly, and I decided to give up. Because if Finn and I didn't get off this beach pretty soon, we'd drown exactly like that poor Jago Jones had obviously done.

'Okay, Finn, have it your way,' I said with my brightest smile. 'So what's the plan now then? I mean, if we don't rescue Shadow and Vixen from the cave, won't the dragon pounce on them too—'

'Oh, no, the dragon's only got a taste for *children's* flesh. Extra tender, see.' Luckily, Finn didn't hear my snort. 'And anyway, they'll both be out soon enough. Those critters are Dragondah born and bred — just like me.'

'Yeah, well, I think bats and foxes are very strange pets to have,' I couldn't help counter sniffily. 'Back home, we had cats and dogs. Although I must admit we did have a pet rat once—'

'Yeah, but Vixen and Shadow aren't my *pets*, Ottillee.' Finn looked most offended. 'They're my friends, my *best* friends. I've known them as far back as I can remember. We look out for each other, see.'

'Oh, right.'

Well, now I'd heard everything. I mean, what an odd boy this Finn was, having animals as best friends rather than other kids. Other kids like — well, *me*, I suppose. And then, I almost jumped out of my skin. Finn had released another whistle, this time louder and shriller than before, although at least he got the result he was after.

First, Vixen raced out of the cave. The fox quickly settled herself at Finn's feet, listening intently as he bent down to whisper something in her ear. Then Shadow soared out, landing on Finn's left shoulder with all the speed and accuracy of a heat-seeking missile.

'Great to see you, old mate!' Finn rewarded the bat with a couple of berries from his pocket. 'We thought you were in big trouble for a minute there, didn't we, Ottillee?'

But I just stepped closer, holding my breath as I took in my first bat. Well, my first *close-up* bat, anyway. Shadow seemed equally curious about me, fixing me with a steady stare that could have been unnerving but wasn't. His warm brown eyes and cute little frown were surprisingly human, as was his squashed nose which was a bit snotty, I couldn't help notice. I watched with fascination as Finn whispered something to him before pulling his pointed ears affectionately.

'Careful!' I yelped when Shadow suddenly bared his fangs, but Finn just chuckled.

'Little scallywag!' he said. 'Hates it when I get all familiar with him, he does. Loves me really though.'

'Sure about that, are you?' I whispered nervously. 'I mean, he's not a vampire bat, is he?'

I could almost swear Shadow bristled at my question. He even bared his fangs at *me*, but Finn carried on regardless.

'Oh, no, this little one's no vampire bat. This little one wouldn't hurt a fly.'

This, as the 'little one' snapped his jaws in the air and swallowed what looked very like a fly.

'Mmmm, he's a bit snotty though, isn't he, Finn? I didn't even know bats could *catch* colds.'

'Me neither, Ottillee, I don't mind admitting. Where the heck he's picked it up, I've no idea. Hey, steady!'

This as Finn was treated to a bat-sized sneeze and a spray of snot. He wasn't bothered, but I stepped backwards to find my bezzie trainers drenched in cold surf. I didn't need to be born and bred in Dragondah to know it was time to get off the beach double-quick. I got no argument for once, and ten minutes later, all four of us were safely back on the clifftop. Finn immediately set off home along the sea path, Vixen trotting happily by his side and Shadow hitching a lift on his cap. I couldn't help grin at the dragonflies twirling and whirling above their heads.

'Hey, Finn!' I yelled with what breath I had left after climbing a hundred steps.

'What's up?'

'Maybe we could see each other again tomorrow, hey?'

'You'd like that?' Finn sounded surprised. Maybe he wasn't quite as cocky as he appeared?

'Sure, I'll come to your place, okay? You're just along the sea path opposite Dragondah Island, right?'

'Yeah, that's where you'll find us, Ottillee. And you can ask Nanna Nessa about Mrs Crow too.'

'Nice one!'

'Oh, and thanks a bunch, by the way.'

'Thanks for what?'

'For my new cap, of course!'

'Oh, erm, yeah, no problem!'

I mean, what else could I say? After all, I had got another baseball cap. And anyway, I was eager to prove my worth to Finn. As eager as I was to join his happy little gang.

—◦◦◇◦◦—

Dad's Secret Report

DATE: Tuesday, 7 August, 2018   TIME: 6:30pm
PLACE: My bedroom   SUBJECT: Life's not in ruins

Dear Dad,

Please ignore my first letter. I know I only wrote it twelve hours ago, but I no longer hate my new home quite so much. In fact, I might even be prepared to give Cornwall another chance. And here's why…

1) Turns out Dragondah <u>is</u> beautiful. Maybe even outstandingly naturally beautiful! It's got ancient woods, and it's got golden beaches, and it's got sparkling waters, even if you do have to put yourself* and your bezzie trainers** in mortal danger to reach them. (There's even talk of an island and a castle, if you can believe it?!) We've also got a cave which is probably nowhere near as big as the one you took me into (with Ella and Dylan for my 8th birthday, remember?), but nobody knows about it yet, so it's still free to go inside!!!

2) The wildlife here is looking up too. And I don't mean the crows, which are still getting on my last nerve. Or the spiders, which are still getting on Mum's. Or the dog, which I still haven't got yet. No, I'm talking about the fox and the bat that I met this morning, both of them as tame as you like!!

3) I'm also fully acclimatised to Dragondah Hall now. My eczema's no worse despite me spending almost two days touching stuff. (Take that, you pesky woodworms!) But I'm not going to tell Mum because she'll make me help with all the cleaning and polishing. And talking of Mum, who knew one of her organic lemon-scented bath bombs could make a bedtime soak so relaxing?

4) Oh, yes, and I've cut down on the time between my bedroom and the kitchen/fridge/biscuits to 4 minutes now. My early mistakes included not turning right by the library (yes, we've got a library!!), not turning left by the dining room (you should see the size of the table in there!!), going up the main staircase (not the back staircase), and getting side-tracked by the empty rooms on the second floor (which look very like the empty rooms on the third floor).

5) Best news of all is there <u>are</u> other people living in Dragondah, and I've got a new friend round about my own age. Mum's delighted, mainly because it gets me out of her hair, I'm thinking! Of course, she might not be <u>so</u> delighted if she knew Finn still believed in dragons. And was a bit snotty about girls. And a bit mean about rough sleepers. But I'm just going to put that down to him growing up in the middle of nowhere.

And not going to school. And not being a girl guide. Oh, yes, and being a boy like you (tee-hee!!!) The most important thing is Finn's very kind to animals. He's also got no family of his own like me. (Well, other than a nanna who sounds a bit like Mum but a better cook.)

6) Finally, what a surprise my benefactress is turning out to be. Seems Mrs Crow was a recluse who spent her days staring unhappily out of upstairs windows instead of knitting, watching telly, and going to garden centres like Mrs Gupta. It makes me really sad to think she had to live her life without people, hobbies, pansies or quiz shows, never mind your wonderful wildlife programmes, Dad. I sort of understand why the poor old lady went a bit doolally now. Although I still don't understand why she turned her back on the rest of the world but not on me!!?!! I mean, it's a total mystery, and I'm only hoping Finn's nan (who's lived round here forever) will be able to help me solve it.

So, that's all from me for now, Dad. Stand by for another Dragondah update soon. Lots of love and a big 'mwah'!!

Your daughter, Ottillee
(AKA the new Mistress of Dragondah Hall!!??!!)

PS: I've found a Cornish dictionary in the library. So, I'm going to teach myself some useful Cornish words, and the first really useful one is 'skogyn', which means half-wit. I also found a tide timetable in there, so there's much less chance of me drowning now.

* Being in 'mortal danger' was a one-time thing, Dad. You don't have to worry about me plummeting to my death as I know exactly where the cliffs are now. Yes, as Mum declared only this morning (having never gone further than the garden), 'It's perfectly safe round these parts.'

** My bezzie trainers are totally useless here. Their soles are too thin, and nearly all the sequins have come off.

I Am Not Doing Anything Dangerous

'CAW! CROAK! CAAAAAAW!'

The speckled crow woke me early again the next morning. Six o'clock early. I lay back against my pillow and considered my surroundings with fresh eyes. I *wanted* to like my new bedroom, honestly I did. After all, Mrs Crow had chosen it specially for me, and I was really trying to respect the wishes of the poor old centenarian recluse.

Sadly though, it wasn't to be. I liked windows, not skylights. Fluffy carpets, not bare floorboards. Wallpaper, not timber frames. Modern pine furniture, not stuffy old antiques. And I was particularly fond of electrical sockets into which I could plug my telly/lamp/handy gadgets.

Yet despite what I'd told Dad yesterday, the posters Mum had stuck up ('Bumstead Rovers Forever' and 'Keep Calm, I'm a Girl Guide') were helping to cheer the place up. So, I snuggled down beneath my duvet and tried to concentrate on all the *other* good things that had happened since I'd arrived in Dragondah.

Finn was right at the top of the list, that was for sure. I mean, yes, he could get on my last nerve with his 'I-know-you're-a-girl' and his 'born-and-bred in Dragondah' nonsense. But really, I'd never met anyone quite like him before — an orphan who knew all about foxes and bats, but hardly anything at all about his own life. I mean, who doesn't know what their last name is, for heaven's sake? And Mum could hardly *believe* he didn't know how old he was!

Yet despite all his little, erm, *oddities*, Finn was still pretty cool, I had to admit. Far too cool to believe in anything as ridiculous as a shapeshifting dragon! In fact, something was telling me that deep down in his soul/stomach/small intestine, Finn suspected the dragon was nothing more than a figment of Nanna Nessa's imagination. Something she'd conjured up to keep him out of Dragondah's dangerous caves when he was a little kid.

So, maybe all Finn needed now was someone to confirm his suspicions were spot on, right? Someone who'd stopped believing in mythical creatures years ago. Someone who already had a whole two hours of caving experience under her belt. Someone who'd managed to find a tide timetable in their library. Someone who knew that high tide was still hours away yet. And someone who might also be quite keen to prove girls were just as good as boys.

I shot up in bed. Because I, Ottillee Bottomly, was that someone. And before I could change my mind, I'd scrambled about my bedroom for suitable cave-exploring gear (black leggings, black sweater, black kagool), checked my scruffy trainers (for spiders), fixed my hair in the bathroom (spit and pigtails), wolfed down a marmalade sandwich, inhaled a chocolate milk, and scribbled a quick note to my mum.

Dear Mum,

Just gone for a healthy morning nature walk.

You'll be pleased to know this is my new hobby.

Back in time for brekkie.

Your daughter Ottillee Bottomly

XXOOXX

PS: Don't worry, I am NOT doing anything dangerous.

PPS: I've taken Dad's Blaze-100 torch

just in case of — well, just in case.

PPPS: Any chance of pancakes for brekkie?

Twenty minutes later, I was back staring over the edge of the cliff. I was also biting my bottom lip, still committed to the task at hand, of course, but also a teensy-weensy bit concerned. A teensy-weensy bit concerned by the storm clouds high above my head. A teensy-weensy bit concerned by the slate grey colour of the distant sea. And a teensy-weensy bit concerned by the strong gusts of wind yanking at my pigtails. I mean, everywhere was still as outstandingly naturally beautiful as yesterday, of course, but it was all a lot darker and wilder and, well — more *threatening* this morning.

But there was no turning back now, of course, so I took a deep breath and set off down the stairway, handling the dodgy four steps like the local expert I'd now become. But as I crossed the stones at the bottom, I couldn't help wonder whether those tiny birds fighting that seagull for food were as crazy as I was? Risking their lives because they were too stupid to realise the danger they were in?

And I don't mind admitting to *serious* second thoughts when I was humming and hawing outside the entrance to the cave. Although who could blame me? Venturing inside a cave was a scary prospect when you were doing it without your dad, or your best friends, or an entry ticket purchased from a kindly old lady. Especially when the cave was rumoured to be the secret lair of a child-eating dragon. And especially when a handful of stones tumbled down the cliff face, only for me to snap my head round and see something flash out of sight.

But then I gave myself another good talking to. Stop being such a lily-livered wimp, Ottillee, I told myself firmly. That was just a crow, that's all that was. And remember what your dad used to say to you when you were little and scared Jesus wanted you for a sunbeam. Or that your armbands had a puncture in them. 'It's okay to be scared, sweetheart,' he'd say while gently dragging me out of the airing cupboard or from the shallow end of the swimming pool. 'Because if you're never scared, how can you ever be brave?'

And bolstered by Dad's wise words, I tightened my grip on his torch and stepped out of the early morning light into the shadowy unknown.

———◇◇◇◇◇———

9

'Who'd Have Believed it?'

'AH-UUH, AAH-UUH, AAAAH-UUUH!'

The sound of heavy breathing was echoing throughout the secret cave. Thankfully though it was only mine, and I continued forward. But I must admit it was taking every ounce of courage I possessed.

What a creepy corner of Dragondah this is, I couldn't help think as I glanced nervously over my shoulder. The smell was nasty, the air was damp, and the light was fading with my every step. I mean, it was little wonder Nanna Nessa had invented the Dragondah dragon because if anything had happened to the young Finn in here, he'd never have been seen again. Why, if anything happened to *me* in here, I'd never be seen again either.

Oh, pooh on a stick! And there was me not even telling Mum where I was going this morning. Never in a million years would she think to look for me down here, and I could only thank my lucky stars that I'd remembered to bring

Dad's torch with me. I shone the Blaze-100 around the cave's surprisingly low and narrow walls, yet a quick flash downwards and the rocky ground was as wet and slimy as I'd imagined. Hey, wait a minute though. *The ground wasn't wet and slimy at all.* A cautious pat confirmed it was bone dry, not a single salty puddle left behind by the outgoing tide.

Golly gosh! Well, *that* was quite the surprise, wasn't it? And I could hardly wait to see the look on Finn's face when I gave him my full report later on. Not only was there no child-eating sea monster skulking away in this cave, but it was also above the high-water mark and therefore perfectly okay for his tramp to live in. (Although surely the poor man could have found somewhere better than *this* freezing-cold hellhole?) And then, just as I decided I'd done enough to dispel Finn's dragon fears while proving how courageous girls were at the same time, I rounded a bend, and my mouth fell open.

An enormous cavern had opened up before me, a cavern so full of shadows, and crevices, and ledges, and boulders that it was impossible to see where it began and where it ended. And that was despite the narrow beam of light shining from somewhere high up in the roof. This sunbeam, just big enough for a single person to stand inside, was so bright and so intense that it didn't seem quite of this world.

I stared at it for a few seconds, aware of nothing but my heart thumping in my chest. Never in my life had I seen anything so — well, *strange*. The light had an almost supernatural feel to it, a supernatural feel that seeped right through my vest to the very marrow in my bones. It was easy to believe something terrifying, otherworldly even, was lurking in the shadows of a place such as this.

I switched off the torch and stayed perfectly still, neither breathing nor moving my eyeballs. Was some strange, cave-dwelling creature about to slither out from behind one of the boulders, I feared? But to my relief, there were no signs of life. (And even more crucial, no signs of death either.)

I stopped holding my breath and started gazing suspiciously all about me. And it was then that I *did* notice something strange. What looked like a bundle of old rags was tucked away on a ledge, a particularly shadowy ledge. I plucked up just enough courage to walk over to it.

'Well, who'd have believed it?' I muttered as I knelt down for a closer look. 'He *is* living in here, after all.'

Because it wasn't a bundle of old rags at all. It was someone's belongings, and they were still very much in use. Next to the tramp's rolled-up sleeping bag was a pillow, a bottle of water, a half-eaten packet of Cornish Creamies biscuits, a bar of soap, a toothbrush and a thick leather-bound book.

I picked up the book without thinking to see it was entitled 'The Dragondah Chronicles'. Then, just as I was about to open the first page, my heart almost leapt from my chest.

'Achooo! Achooo! Cough-cough! Achooo! Achoooo! Cough! Achoo! Cough-cough-cough!'

Oh, blithering barnacles, as Finn would say! The tramp had just entered the cave, and although I'd boasted about my own friendship with Bumstead Billy, I must admit I was rigid with fear. I mean, as much as I'd tried to stick up for rough sleepers, I'd never set eyes on this particular one, had I? He could easily be the nasty piece of work Finn claimed he was. And a nasty piece of work was sure to get even nastier when he found a stranger rifling through his personal belongings. A stranger who was all alone.

'Achooo! Achooo!'

In a state of near panic, I dropped the book and raced over to a particularly large boulder. Slipping behind it, I did all I could to control my ragged breathing while deciding what to do next. Although what *I* did next largely depended upon what the tramp did next.

He might go back outside, of course, allowing me to make my escape and join Mum in time for breakfast pancakes. But it was far more likely that he'd lie down on his sleeping bag, tuck into a Cornish Creamie, notice his book wasn't where he'd left it, poke about with suspicious eyes, find my hiding place and — well, what happened next wasn't worth thinking about.

Oh, pooh on a stick, I couldn't help think to myself, I've got myself in a right pickle now, haven't I? And I had no one to blame but myself. I mean, Finn had warned me to steer clear of the cave *and* the tramp, now I came to think about it. But there was me thinking I knew better. Just because I'd wanted to prove London girls were as good as Cornish boys. And just because I was a bossy-boots outsider who thought she knew better than everyone else.

Well, look where my snotty attitude had got me this morning, hey? Cowering in a cave waiting for heaven knew what to happen, that's where. I scratched hard at my neck, agonizing over what to do next. Probably one of the following...

1. Say hi to the man who'd offer me a Cornish Creamie before waving me merrily on my way.
2. Race past the man and get to Dragondah Hall before he got to me.
3. Say hi to the man and never be heard from again.
4. Wait it out until I died of hunger, thirst or loneliness.

Not happy with my chances of the first two happening, I glanced over my shoulder in the desperate hope another option would magically present itself. Well, what an incredible bit of luck. It had! A tunnel was winding its way deeper into the rock behind me. A dark and narrow tunnel but with walls so perfectly arched that they must have been hollowed out by man rather than by nature. Although when I heard the slow but unmistakable sound of footsteps on stone, I didn't care if the tunnel had been hollowed out by the shapeshifting dragon itself. I turned around and started walking.

———◦◇◇◦———

10

'Cripes!'

I HURRIED ALONG the tunnel, praying I'd reach the way out soon. Fine cobwebs attached themselves to my hair. Musty odours assaulted my nostrils. Odd sounds reached my ears as I kicked over — well, who the heck knew? And while random pinpricks of light were all that was saving me from total darkness, I was too scared to shine my torch for longer than a few panicky flashes. Because what if Finn's tramp was after me, hey? What then? I mean, nobody would find my rotting corpse for years. If ever.

Then, just as I was imagining myself as the new Jago Jones and a dire warning to all know-it-all outsiders everywhere, I shone my torch and spotted something ahead. It was an iron gate through which I could make out a narrow flight of steps carved into the rock. A little white door was waiting at the top of them.

I hurried forward, hardly able to believe my luck when

the gate opened, never mind with the screech of something that hadn't been opened for years. And then my eyes widened even further. I could hear someone laughing on the other side of the white door. And even more astonishing, I was sure I'd heard that laugh somewhere before.

I made my way up the steps, sighing with relief when the door opened with only the gentlest of pushes. I stepped through it and found myself in a small room lined with shelves full of stuff. Stuff like sauce bottles, soup tins, baked bean tins and wine bottles, as well as jars of everything from peanut butter to strawberry jam. There were at least two rows of stinky cheeses, and enough kitchen rolls and toilet rolls to wallpaper a house. There was even one whole shelf devoted to toiletries like organic lemon-scented bath bombs and Gorgeous-Girl hair serum. Art supplies, everything from paints and brushes to different-sized canvases, were piled high in one corner.

'Cripes!' I gasped as everything suddenly fell into place. Although even now, I could hardly believe I'd found myself back at Dragondah Hall. That the tunnel had wound its way beneath the woods to the kitchen pantry of my very own home. And that the laughter I could hear belonged to my very own mother! But who the heck was making her chortle away like she hadn't done in months? Like only my dad had been able to make her do?

A frown creased my forehead as I squinted through a

crack in the pantry door. A large man in a grey business suit was sitting with his back to me at the head of our kitchen table. Mum was pouring him what looked like a coffee, and to my horror, she was pouring it into Dad's special Bumstead Rovers mug.

I don't mind admitting my eyes nearly popped out of my head. For a kick-off, it was far too early for uninvited guests. Half-past eight according to the kitchen clock opposite. (Mum hadn't even brushed her hair and was still in her dressing gown, for heaven's sake!) And how *dare* she let this man, who didn't know Dad and probably wasn't even a Bumstead Rovers supporter, guzzle coffee from our most precious possession?

Careless of the consequences, I marched out of the pantry and plonked myself down at the opposite end of the table, straight-backed, stony-faced and with my eyes burning holes in the mug.

'Oh, bless my soul, Ottillee, where did *you* spring from?' Mum shot round, and I couldn't help notice her cheeks flush pink with guilt. 'Back already, are you?'

The most I could manage was a shrug.

'Well, go on, Ottillee, where are your manners?' Mum let out a strange, tinkling laugh. 'Say hello to Mr Branson here, Mr Lucifer Branson. He's moving to the area himself soon and has just stopped by to introduce himself. Now, isn't that absolutely charming of him?'

I mumbled hello, but continued to glare at Dad's mug. Anything to avoid meeting the eyes of this — this *intruder*. I mean, how dare he sit at the head of our table? And how dare he charm my mother? (Who was far too nice for her own good.) But my silence only made matters worse because Mum now dragged *me* into their conversation.

'Yes, Ottillee, I was just telling Lucifer that you'd gone on a nature walk this morning.'

Continued glowering from me (*Lucifer*, I mean, really!), but the man didn't take the hint.

'Yes, that's very commendable of you, young lady,' he said pleasantly. 'Especially in such inclement weather. So, tell me, how did you fare on this nature walk of yours?'

Yes, the man was doing his best to charm *me* now, his voice deep yet also warm and friendly. In fact, his voice was *so* warm and friendly that even *I* knew I couldn't ignore it for much longer.

I lifted my gaze and did my best to hide my dismay. Crikey, Lucifer Branson was about as warm and friendly as a bird of prey. His hair was too black, his teeth were too white, his suit was too shiny, and his grip on Dad's mug was too tight. A flashy gold watch was glinting on his hairy wrist. Yet what *really* unnerved me about our uninvited visitor were his cold and calculating eyes. Or should I say 'eye'? Because one of them (I was hoping the kind and gentle one) was covered with a black leather patch.

'Yes, my nature walk was very, erm, fine,' I managed to get out, uncomfortably aware that I was staring at the eye patch rather rudely. But no matter how far forward I leaned, no matter how hard I squinted, I couldn't work out what the little white symbol in the middle of it was supposed to represent.

'Very fine, hey?' Lucifer Branson smirked at me as though he knew exactly what I was up to. 'And did you go far on this *very fine* nature walk of yours?'

'Oh, no, just through the woods and down to the beach.'

I shrugged carelessly, expecting this to be the end of our conversation. But it was as if Lucifer Branson sensed I was hiding something.

'So, let me see what you brought back with you, young lady. Any pretty feathers or rare seashells? Any dried dragonfly wings?' His voice dropped to a whisper. 'Or even better, what about some dried animal dung?'

'Oh, erm, no,' I stuttered, struggling to explain my lack of interesting finds. 'I seem to have dropped my — erm, dried animal dung somewhere on the way back.'

Even I knew how stupid *that* sounded. It was no surprise when Lucifer Branson tossed my mum a knowing glance.

'Got her head in the clouds, this one, hasn't she, Grace?' he said with another lofty smile. 'Exactly like my own daughter, truth be told. She's eleven too.'

I very nearly fainted when Mum rushed to my defence.

'Oh, no, Lucifer, my Ottillee's not the daydreaming sort at all,' she insisted with touching loyalty. 'She's been very busy since we got to Dragondah. In fact, she was out and about yesterday getting to know the locals.'

'The locals, hey?' Lucifer Branson's smile slipped, only to return even wider and whiter than before. 'And what — erm, locals would these be, Grace?'

'Oh, this was just some boy by the name of Flynn, wasn't it, Ottillee?'

'*Finn*,' I corrected tightly, still trying to get over all the 'Lucifers' and 'Graces' that were being tossed around the kitchen. This man had only known us for five minutes, for heaven's sake.

'And what was this local boy's *last* name?' the man asked, only for Mum to jump in again.

'Well, you'll hardly credit it, Lucifer, but he doesn't even know! He's an orphan, you see.'

'Is that so?' Lucifer Branson's cold and calculating eye narrowed on me. He leant forward as if he didn't want to miss a single word I said. 'And whereabouts in Dragondah does this unfortunate waif and stray live, did you say?'

'I didn't say,' I muttered. 'In fact, I've no idea.'

Lucifer Branson was suddenly far too curious about Finn for my liking. Even he seemed to realise he'd overstepped the mark and relaxed back in his seat.

'To be honest with you, Grace,' he said after a few

more sips of coffee from Dad's mug, 'I didn't even know Dragondah *had* any locals — well, apart from you two lovely ladies, of course.'

'Oh, Lucifer, how nice of you to say so.'

I frowned at Mum. Honestly, couldn't she see how — how *inappropriate* this Lucifer Branson was? Giving us smarmy compliments? Asking us nosy questions? I shot her a warning glance, and thankfully she got the message.

'Anyway, Lucifer, thanks so much for taking the time to introduce yourself to us today,' she said, practically tugging Dad's mug out of his hand. 'And you really must stop by again soon. You know, when Ottillee and I are both a bit more settled.'

Fortunately, Lucifer Branson took the hint this time. He got to his feet with a brief glance at his watch.

'Yes, of course, Grace. Time I was going anyway.' His smile was a bit too long and lingering for my liking. 'And once again, I'm so sorry I never caught any of your husband's wildlife documentaries. For too busy for TV, I'm afraid.'

Mum smiled back. 'Oh, that's okay, Lucifer.'

'But I will accept your invitation to drop by again soon. After all, we blow-ins must stick together—'

'Blow-ins?'

'Yes, didn't you know, Grace? That's what the locals call people who are new to Cornwall. People like the three of us.'

And with this, Lucifer Branson took a business card out of his top pocket and placed it on the table. I waited until Mum was showing him to the front door before I picked it up.

———◦◦◇◦◦———

'There's Something Shifty Going On.'

OH, SO LUCIFER BRANSON was a stamp collector, was he? How strange, because everyone knows stamp collectors (like my friend Dylan) aren't the sort of people to wear leather eye patches or charm mothers while they were still in their nighties. Lucifer Branson's business card also had a P.O. Box number on it rather than a proper address, as well as the same puzzling symbol I'd spotted on his eye patch.

I placed the card back on the table with a heavy sigh. Somehow, and I'm not exactly sure why, I was finding Lucifer Branson's sudden appearance in our lives very troubling. And not just because of his nosiness. Or his pushiness. Or even his smarminess. No, it was because of his — well, total *phoniness*. I poured Nutty Granola into my bowl, too rattled to admit I'd picked up Mouldy Muesli by mistake. (That's what I called it anyway.)

'Oh, Ottillee, please don't eat my cereal.' Mum's rebuke

was gentle as she returned to the kitchen. 'You know you're not that keen, and I've already started on the pancake mix.'

But I continued stuffing the birdseed into my mouth.

'Come on, Ottillee, you asked for pancakes, didn't you?'

I ignored her and kept on chewing.

'DID YOU HEAR ME, YOUNG LADY?'

I finally met Mum's frustrated gaze.

'*What?*'

'Pancakes, Ottillee, I'm making you pancakes!' She was standing by the cooker waving a bowl of batter around. 'And take your elbows off the table, for heaven's sake!'

'But I don't *want* any pancakes, Mum.' I slammed down my spoon and scowled across the room at her. 'I don't want any food at all. In fact, I've totally lost my appetite.'

And now it was Mum's turn to scowl across the room. 'Oh, really, Ottillee, I know what this is all about, and there's absolutely no need for you to get in such a tizz over our visitor, you know. I was just being friendly, that's all.'

'Oh, *friendly*, was it? Letting him drink out of Dad's mug like that?'

Without waiting for an answer, I got up and deliberately made quite a production of washing the mug in the sink, scrubbing it extra hard and humming the *Wilderness World* theme tune while I was at it. When I placed the mug back on the dresser, next to our favourite photo of Dad like the family treasure it was, Mum shook her head tiredly.

'As I said, Ottillee, I really don't have the patience for any more of your childish antics this morning.' She turned away to pour the batter into the pan. 'Now, do you want three pancakes or four?'

But I wasn't joking when I said I'd lost my appetite. I could still hear Mum gossiping with Lucifer Branson, and it only stiffened my resolve.

'You shouldn't have said anything to that man about Finn, you know,' I said. 'I mean, it's none of his business where he lives. *Or* what his last name is, is it?'

'Oh, nonsense, Ottillee, where's the harm in it? Lucifer was just showing an interest in his new neighbours, that's all. And I, for one, am grateful for his fresh take on things.' She glanced briefly at me over her shoulder. 'How Mrs Crow first found out about you and your dad, for example.'

'What do you mean?'

'Well, I don't know why we didn't think of it ourselves, Ottillee. Because if Mrs Crow didn't watch Ross on the telly—'

'—which she couldn't have done because she didn't *have* a telly—'

'—then she must have read about him in the national newspapers, mustn't she? And that's obviously how she found out about you too, sweetheart. There were certainly plenty of photos of you at your dad's memorial service, remember?'

But I didn't *want* to remember that terrible time. And my dismay over Mum discussing such personal things with a stranger must have shown on my face.

'No, don't look like that, Ottillee. I was just making polite conversation with Lucifer, that's all. You know how flustered I can get when I meet new people.' Mum avoided my gaze because she knew I was right. But then a few more swirls of the pancake batter, and she stuck up for herself. 'Although why shouldn't I make some new friends down here? You've already got yourself a new friend in Finn, haven't you?'

'Yeah, Mum, but there's something very dodgy about that man, let me tell you. There's something shifty going on behind his eyes. Or should I say "eye"?'

'Don't be clever, Ottillee.'

'And did you see that swanky gold watch on his wrist?' I picked up the business card and walked over to her. 'How can a stamp collector afford something like that?'

'A stamp collector?' Mum took the card and read it with a frown. 'Lucifer's a philanthropist, I see.'

'Yeah, I mean Dylan's a phip — a philap — I mean one of those, and he could never buy himself an expensive watch like that. In fact, he never stops moaning about how much the stamps *themselves* cost him.'

A shriek of laughter now. 'Oh, honestly, sweetheart, I can't believe what you come out with sometimes. Stamp collectors like Dylan are *phil-at-el-ists*.' Mum pronounced the word very distinctly as if I was hard of hearing. 'Whereas *phil-an-throp-ists* like Lucifer are — well, they're do-gooders, that's what they are. They've made so much money in their lives that they very kindly give quite a bit of it away to charity. They're two very different things.'

Oh, pooh, I could have kicked myself.

'Yes, Ottillee, you shouldn't be so quick to judge people, you know. You only have to look at Lucifer Branson to know he's a very decent and honourable man. '

Humph! I only had to look at Lucifer Branson to know he was a very devious and horrible man. But my too-trusting Mum had already made up her mind about him, so what was the point of arguing?

I'd just have to be careful what I told her in future. In case she got all flustered and found herself making 'polite conversation' again. For example, there was no way I was going to tell her about the secret tunnel now. Or about the tramp living in the cave. Or about my mission to find out more about Mrs Crow. I mean, how the old lady first found out about me was no one else's business, was it? Certainly not dodgy strangers like Lucifer Branson's.

'Anyway, Ottillee, I'll ask you again,' I heard Mum say now, 'do you want three pancakes or four?'

'I don't want *any* pancakes, Mum. I've — well, I've decided to go over to Finn's instead.'

'In this weather?' Mum nodded towards the window with raised eyebrows.

I followed her gaze but nodded back. I mean, what was a spot of rain after what I'd already been through this Wednesday morning?

'So Finn *invited* you over to his house today, did he?' she double-checked. 'And you know where it is?'

'Course, I do, Mum — so that's okay, is it?'

'Well, I'd feel happier if I could meet this boy first.'

'Why?' I sighed heavily. 'Because he's an orphan who doesn't know what his last name is?'

'Of course not, Ottillee. But I do know all your other friends, so why not him?'

'Okay.' I got to my feet and met her gaze. 'If it makes you feel any better, I'll ask Finn round to the house. Tomorrow if you like?'

'That's my girl.' Mum's smile wavered when she looked me up and down. 'But don't you think you should tidy yourself up a bit if you're making a social call? You've got dirt on your cheeks, and your pigtails are all skew-whiff — help yourself to some of my Gorgeous-Girl hair serum, if you like. And why don't you swap that scruffy old kagool for your smart red mac?'

'Aw, *mu-umm*.'

'Yes, Ottillee, I can't help thinking you look like a mini-ninja dressed all in black like that. And we wouldn't want

Finn's parents to think they were under some sort of attack now, would we?'

I didn't even smile at Mum's little joke. Neither did I remind her that Finn didn't *have* any parents. I simply shrugged, zipped up my kagool and made my escape.

———◦◦◊◦◦———

12

'Piddledowndidda To You Too!'

I STOMPED ALONG the sea path towards Finn's house with my hood up and my head down. I was hardly aware of the worsening weather or the screeching seagulls. All I could think about was Mum and her snotty attitude towards me.

Because even she'd been an 11-year-old girl once in her life, hadn't she? (Before she'd turned into a 35-year-old gossip who let strange men drink out of totally inappropriate mugs.) I mean, why did she always dismiss *my* take on things? Why did she always treat me like a child? Honestly, never in my life had I felt so alone. Never in my life had I missed my dad so much. Because he'd always listened to what I had to say—

And then I rounded a bend and spotted something that wiped even Dad from my mind.

The unmistakable shape of a castle was rising up from a rocky little island far out in the bay. Surrounded by the choppy grey water of the incoming tide, its high stone walls were just about visible through the heavy rain that was now falling out at sea. And while Finn had already told me that Dragondah had its own castle, he'd never told me it was quite so big or quite so thrilling either. I mean, had his dragon been soaring about its tower that very moment, I don't think I'd have batted an eyelid.

And talking of Finn, hadn't he said he lived somewhere round here? I peered about me with increasing frustration, but there were no houses anywhere to be seen. Just a large field with a munching rabbit and another speckled crow. (The crow was probably waiting for the cute little bunny to choke on a dandelion.) Then suddenly, I heard a yell.

'Hey, you, Ottillee Violet Rose Bottomly!'

I grinned with relief as a familiar baseball cap, closely followed by a familiar face, popped up behind the low stone wall at the edge of the field. I was so pleased to see Finn that I didn't even bother to tell him he'd got my middle names the wrong way round.

'So, where's your house then?' I yelled back, careless that I was getting properly rained on now. Although I did know that I was suddenly feeling a whole lot better, and eager to recount my early morning adventures.

But Finn's face vanished as quickly as it had appeared. 'Who said I lived in a *house?*' was his parting cry, leaving me little option but to race across the grass and peer over the wall.

'Well, what do you know?' I muttered under my breath, again astonished by the sight that met my eyes.

Because secreted away in a hollow beneath an over-hanging tree wasn't a house but a van. Actually, it was more like a horsebox, although quite a bit bigger than Olivia McDonald's 'pony' horsebox back in Bumstead. This one was made out of wood and had four windows along the side and a driver's cab at the front. Smoke was rising from its narrow chimney, a vegetable plot was thriving nearby, and a bicycle was propped up against the handy freshwater tap that was poking out of the ground. It was no surprise when Finn stuck his head through the top section of the door.

'There's cake in here, Ottillee!' he cried. 'And it's really starting to bucket down now. Come *on*, will you!'

I didn't need telling twice and cleared the wall with all the agility of any 11-year-old mini-ninja. Seconds later, I was stepping into Finn's surprisingly spacious home and being greeted by a toothless old lady in a floral dress and spotted headscarf. She was sitting at a table laid out with what looked and smelt like freshly baked treats.

'Just in time, girly!' said Nanna Nessa, trying to make herself heard over the rain now pounding on the roof. 'Piddledowndidda!'

'Piddledowndidda to you too!' I said just as loudly before wiping my face and wringing out my pigtails. (I hadn't the first clue what 'piddledowndidda' meant, of course, but I knew it was the best word I'd heard since 'willy-nilly'.)

Finn's mobile home was a revelation too, and my eyes were wide as I looked all about me. A built-in table with bench seating. A tiny cooking range with a sink. And a narrow door leading to some sort of bathroom facilities, I supposed. There were also two bunk beds at the far end, and Finn was currently perched on the bottom one tucking into what looked like a pastry. Vixen's head was on his lap, her eyes fixed and her nose twitching.

Mouthwatering smells were also drifting towards my own nostrils, and I realised the account of my morning's adventures would just have to wait for now.

'Oh, how I'd *love* to live somewhere like this,' I said as I accepted Nanna Nessa's invitation to sit down opposite her. I shrugged off my wet kagool and continued gazing all about me, taking in the wood-panelled walls, the mismatched cushions, the shelves groaning with books, and the brightly-coloured curtains adorning the steamed-up windows. And then I realised something. 'Don't you miss having a telly though, Nanna Nessa? I know I do.'

'Oh, no, no tellies for us, Ottillee. Finn and I are too busy living our *own* lives to watch other folks living theirs.' Nanna Nessa chuckled as she handed me a plate. 'Now, get one of my figgy 'obbins down you — fresh out of the oven, they are.'

I accepted the delicious-looking pastry, not just to satisfy my hunger but also to hide my surprise. I mean, didn't anyone in this part of the world own a television? Didn't anyone want to enjoy award-winning programmes like my dad's *Wilderness World?* It was as though everyone in Dragondah was perfectly content living in their *own* little wilderness world! I glanced over at Finn to get his reaction, but he was far too busy sharing his pastry with Vixen. I couldn't help smile when I saw what was hanging on a hook above his head. The red baseball cap had pride of place.

'Don't worry about that one over there, girly — keep eating!'

I did as Nanna Nessa ordered, sneaking quick looks at her over the top of my figgy 'obbin. And the old lady was certainly worth looking at, let me tell you. I mean, I'd never seen anyone so wrinkly in my whole life. In fact, Nanna Nessa's face had more wrinkles in it than it did actual face! Wispy strands of white hair were peeping out from beneath her headscarf, and there didn't appear to be a tooth left in her head. But her cheeks were as plump and rosy as a pair of apples, and her blue eyes were still twinkling like a mischievous young girl's.

'So, how you liking it, child?' Nanna Nessa was able to talk more normally now that the rain was easing off. She was also watching me closely as I chomped away on her pastry. 'And can I get you a nettle tea to wash that down with?'

'Erm—'

'Or would a regular cuppa suit you better?'

'Oh, no, don't trouble yourself, Nanna Nessa. But this, erm, cake is absolutely delish.'

A raisin suddenly flew out of my mouth, only for the old lady to pick it off the rug with a chuckle.

'Waste not, want not!' she cried, swallowing the raisin with a satisfied smack of her lips and a glance over her shoulder. I glanced round too, and couldn't help gasp with surprise. Shadow was hanging from a brass perch in the corner of the van, upside down and apparently fast asleep.

'Don't bother about that one either, Ottillee!' said Nanna Nessa. 'Shadow's just had himself half a banana, so dead to the world, he is. Best place for him too!'

I smiled at her little joke (at least, I *think* it was a joke) and scratched hard at my eczema. I was a bit nervous, I'll admit, and not just because the old lady's piercing blue eyes were still fixed upon me. No, I was wondering whether this was the best time for me to quiz her about my benefactress. But to my surprise, she raised the subject herself.

'So, young lady, I hear Cowenna Crow has made you the new mistress of Dragondah Hall?'

'That's right.' I nodded in a helpless, almost embarrassed sort of way. 'Problem is, I've no idea *why* though.'

'Yes, Finn told me you'd never met her?'

'Yes, it's true. I never met her in my whole life. I mean, she was *supposed* to have been a fan of my dad's wildlife programmes, but that can't have been true.'

'Why not?'

'Because she was just like you, and didn't have a telly either. I mean, Mum's *now* thinking that Mrs Crow saw photos of me in the newspapers — you know, at my dad's memorial service back in London. Although this still doesn't explain why she left me all her worldly goods, of course. Unless she just felt sorry for me.' I clawed at my neck, wondering how to continue this conversation without causing offence. '*I'm* just wondering whether the poor old lady was such an old, erm, you know—'

'Fossil?'

'Yes.' I couldn't help smile at Nanna Nessa's frankness. 'That maybe she'd gone a bit, erm—'

'Doolally?'

'Yeah, sort of.'

'Whiffle-headed?'

'Mmmm.'

'Mad as a box of frogs?'

'Yeah, that *is* what I'm starting to think.' I smiled again. 'You know, maybe the old lady got so confused towards the end of her life that she actually thought she *did* know me—'

Suddenly there was a muffled sneeze behind me, closely followed by a steady squeaking sound. I swung round to see Shadow's perch swinging back and forth as though the bat was now awake and listening in on our conversation. Nanna Nessa took advantage of the interruption to reach onto a shelf and produce a small, round tin.

'Why don't you take some of this ointment back home with you, girly? Very good for skin complaints, it is, and I must say that eczema on your neck looks quite tender.'

Touched by the old lady's kindness, I smiled my thanks and stuffed the tin in my pocket.

'Anyway, Nanna Nessa, you've lived in Dragondah for ages and ages, haven't you?' I did my best to ignore the squeaking perch. 'Do you think I could be right about Mrs Crow? I mean, I don't really know anything about her, other than she was a recluse—'

'Humph!' The old lady banged the table so hard that the plate of figgy 'obbins jumped in the air. 'Cowenna Crow was no recluse, Ottillee. She was an outcast more like!'

'An *outcast?*'

I gasped with shock. Oh, my poor benefactress. Being an outcast was far worse than being a recluse. At least recluses *chose* to be alone, whereas outcasts had it forced upon them.

'Yes, like I told this one last night—' Nanna Nessa patted Finn's hand as he squeezed himself in around the table, 'the moment Cowenna moved into Dragondah Hall, she brought all her misfortunes upon herself.'

'But how the heck did she do *that?*'

I was vaguely aware that Shadow's swing had finally fallen silent, and that even the rain had stopped. It was as if Nanna Nessa was about to reveal something shocking, although *how* shocking I'd no idea.

'Cowenna brought everlasting shame to her family,' the old lady continued bleakly. 'Broke their hearts, she did.'

'But *how?*' I glanced over at Finn in confusion. 'Finn did say she was a bit giddy when she was younger, but—'

'Humph! Giddiness was one of Cowenna's *good* points, Ottillee. No, it was her wilfulness that was her downfall in the end. I was still a babe in arms, of course, so got all this information second-hand. But according to my sister, no one could stop Cowenna doing exactly what she wanted to do.'

'Yes, but what did she actually *do* though?' I was really hoping my benefactress hadn't murdered anyone.

Although she might as well have done for all the venom in Nanna Nessa's reply.

'She got wed, Ottillee, that's what she did.' Her eyes were dark with bitterness. 'She got wed to Judas Crow when she was nothing but a slip of a girl. Just turned seventeen she had—'

'But that's not so bad, is it?' I cried indignantly. 'Lots of people get married when they're young. I mean, my mum was only eighteen herself. Couldn't wait to marry Dad, she said—'

'Yes, but did your mum pledge herself to a man with a heart as black as coal?'

'Well, no—'

'Did she tie herself to a family that had brought nothing but the greatest shame to Cornwall? A family that her own kith and kin had been feuding with for nigh on a thousand years?' Now another expression appeared on Nanna Nessa's face, something like satisfaction. 'Although Cowenna got her comeuppance in the end, didn't she? Judas Crow abandoned her soon as look at her, and she spent the next eighty years of her life alone.'

'Eighty years *alone?*'

'Indeed, girly. No one round here visited Judas Crow's wife if they could help it. Word was a girl drove over from Chuggypig once a month to stock up her pantry and dust about a bit. Her gardener dropped by more regularly, of course. And Doctor Denzel attended her at the end.' A sniff. 'And it was lucky he did, Ottillee, or else Cowenna would have been left rotting in her bed for weeks on end.'

'Oh, the poor woman,' I muttered, upset by such a horrifying image. Although at least I now understood why Mrs Crow hadn't left her home to anyone round here, not least her heartless family.

'You've got to understand the rules are different in this part of the world,' said Nanna Nessa, sensing my disquiet. 'Dragondah's long been a battleground between the forces of good and evil. And believe me, it wouldn't take much for us all to be plunged into darkness again.'

'Plunged into *darkness?*' I breathed with a nervous glance at Finn.

'Yeah, Nan, don't put the wind up Ottillee! Those days are long gone, right?'

Nanna Nessa considered Finn for a moment, as though she wasn't quite ready to give Dragondah the all-clear yet.

'Mmmm, just be careful who you trust round here,' was all she finally conceded with a sniff. 'Some people might not be *quite* who they seem to be, that's all I'm saying.'

And with this, all hell broke loose. Shadow flew off his perch, bared his fangs at Nanna Nessa and flew around the horsebox like a crazy thing. Curtains flew, books fell, pans swung, and Finn and Nanna Nessa started yelling at each other in Cornish. Finn finally leapt up to open the door, only for the bat to soar through it with the speed of a budgie let out of its cage for the first time.

Finn darted after him, immediately followed by the faithful Vixen. I grabbed my kagool and was about to set off in hot pursuit when I felt a restraining hand on my arm. Nanna Nessa's grip was uncomfortably tight, and I turned to find her blue eyes burning into mine.

'You're right to question your inheritance, girly,' the old lady whispered urgently. 'But you're wrong about Cowenna Crow feeling sorry for you—'

'I am?'

'Yes, tough as old boots, that one was. She'd never have left her beloved Dragondah Hall to some heartbroken London girl on little more than a whim and a fancy.'

'She wouldn't?'

'No, and as for Cowenna's state of mind, Doctor Denzil saw her regularly in the weeks before she died. He assured me she was as sharp as a tack right up to her very last breath.'

Silence as I struggled to digest this startling new piece of information.

'Then if Mrs Crow *was* as sharp as a tack,' I finally said, 'that means she chose me to take over Dragondah Hall for a reason.'

'Yes, a good and proper reason, child.'

'But what the heck was it?'

'I've no idea, girly. Just keep digging, and the truth will out in the end.' The old lady released my arm and smiled her gummy smile. 'All that concerns *me* right now is whether you'll help my Finn?'

'*Help* him?'

'Yes, I've mollycoddled the boy too much over the years, I'll admit. Told him white lies to keep him safe and happy, and hidden shocking truths from him for exactly the same reason.'

I nodded, even though I hadn't a clue what she was talking about.

'Yes, child, you already know how harsh this world can be, don't you? Finn told me about your dad.'

'I suppose.'

'Yes, you've had to grow up very quickly these past two years, no doubt about it. My boy just needs to catch up with you, that's all—'

'Catch *up* with me?'

'Yes, because Finn's about to come face to face with his destiny.'

'His *destiny?*'

'Yes, and then his carefree childhood will be well and truly over. Just like yours was well and truly over the day your poor father met his end.' Nanna Nessa pulled a thin blue anorak off the back of the door and held it out to me. 'So, can I rely on you to be a good friend to my boy?'

'Yes, yes — erm, of course you can.'

I took Finn's anorak and managed to smile at Nanna Nessa before setting off down the steps. I managed to smile even though her hints and warnings were as disturbing as they were baffling. And something was telling me the old lady was *still* keeping something from me. Something important.

13

'Who Owns That Castle, Finn?'

FINN AND VIXEN were standing at the edge of the cliff gazing out across the bay. Dragondah Castle was clearly visible now that the rain had stopped, its rocky island home surrounded by the rolling grey waters of the incoming tide. The castle had a desolate air about it, I couldn't help think as I hurried across the soaking-wet grass. As if it had been battling Cornwall's pounding surf for centuries and suspected no one would notice if it gave up the ghost.

'Who owns that castle, Finn?' I asked as I joined him at the cliff edge.

'Not a clue, Ottillee. Nan could probably tell you more if you're interested?'

'Oh, no, no need for that.' The last thing I wanted was another conversation with Nanna Nessa. I was eager to put her disturbing predictions about darkness and destiny behind me. 'So Shadow's disappeared again, has he? Flown over to the castle, do you think?'

'Who knows? Honestly, the little feller never used to go off like this during the day.' Finn accepted the anorak from me with a wry grin. 'I'm beginning to think his odd behaviour has got something to do with *you*, Ottillee!'

'Oh, yeah, sure!' I grinned back. 'Anyway, please try not to worry. Shadow will be back home with you and your nan soon enough, I'm sure. And in the meantime, I've got loads of stuff I want to tell you.'

I was desperate to fill Finn in on my early-morning adventures. And once I'd got going, I couldn't stop. I didn't miss anything out either. Not the dry-as-a-bone cave. Not the tramp. Not the book. Not the biscuits. Not the secret tunnel. Not even the smarmy cheek of Mum's new friend Lucifer Branson. And encouraged by Finn's increasingly wide-eyed shock, I ended with a showy little twirl to emphasise that I hadn't been eaten by any dragons either. But this got a very different response.

'Yeah, well, that's no surprise.' Finn's gaze shifted away from me.

'Isn't it?'

'Nope.'

'But only yesterday you were insisting that a shapeshifting dragon lived—'

'Yeah, but that was before—'

'Before what? Come on, Finn, why are you being so shifty?'

'I'm being shifty because last night—' he released a heavy sigh, 'Nan *finally* confessed that she'd made the whole dragon thing up. And that Dragondah *was* most likely named after the dragonflies. Probably swarms of them round here back in the day, she said. And I must admit, they *still* seem very fond of our rock pools.'

I managed to swallow the words 'I told you so', and tutted at the deviousness of grown-ups instead.

'Yeah, exactly, Ottillee. Nan was just trying to scare me, that's all. She was worried about me getting lost inside the caves when I was a nipper, see.' Finn was understandably keen to change the subject. 'Actually, she told me some other interesting stuff too—'

'About Cowenna Crow? Yeah, I know—'

'No, not just about Mrs Crow. About Dragondah Hall back in the olden days.'

'Oh, my gosh, Finn, like what? Come on, tell me.'

Despite my urging, I was starting to feel uneasy again. I mean, Nanna Nessa never seemed to share any *good* news, did she? And it didn't help that Finn was looking at me as though I'd be sure to collapse with shock at his revelations. I very nearly did.

'Well, it turns out that Dragondah Hall was once the wickedest place in all of Cornwall.'

'*What?*' Now I really was feeling shaken. I mean, this was my new home Finn was talking about.

'Yeah, and it was all down to Judas Crow and his ancestors—'

'Judas Crow? You mean the Judas Crow who married *my* Cowenna? The Judas Crow with the heart as black as coal?'

'Yeah, the very same. Nan said the Crows were the scourge of Cornwall back in the day. Real wrong 'uns they were, prepared to murder anyone who got in their way.'

'And these horrid people lived in my house?'

'They didn't just live in your house, Ottillee, they *built* your house!'

'Oh, for heaven's sake!'

'Yes, the Crows really wanted to live in Dragondah Castle, of course. Plotted and schemed like mad to get their hands on it, Nan said—'

'Plotted and schemed against who?'

'Oh, Nan was a bit vague about that.' Finn nodded out to sea. 'But you've got to admit that the castle would make the perfect hideout for wreckers and smugglers like them.'

'*Reckless* smugglers? Cripes!'

'No, wreckers *and* smugglers, Ottillee.' Finn's eyes narrowed on me. 'You do know what wreckers used to get up to in the olden days, don't you?'

'Of *course* I know what wreckers used to get up to in the olden days. They used to, erm—'

Finn finally gave up waiting for me to come up with something suitably wicked.

'They used to wreck ships.'

'Ships?'

'Yes, they used to use fake lights to lure the ships onto the rocks far out at sea. And then the wreckers would go on board, kill all the survivors—' Finn made a savage slicing motion against his throat, 'and steal all their gold jewellery and stuff.'

'You're kidding me?' This was even worse than I'd imagined. 'No wonder Cowenna's family were so against her marrying Judas Crow. Was he a wrecker too?'

'No, wrecking had died out by Judas's time, so he became a smuggler. Or rather the *king* of smugglers, Nan said. Ruled this coastline with a rod of iron, he did, making sure he got his cut from all the stuff smuggled across the water into Cornwall. You know, fancy stuff like tobacco from America, and silk from China, and tea leaves from India—'

'Cripes!' My eyes grew wide with dismay as something suddenly occurred to me. 'Nutmeg and ginger too?'

'Why do you say that?'

'Because I've just realised that the Crows named the bedrooms at Dragondah Hall after all their smuggled stuff!'

'You're kidding me?'

'No, we've got a "Tobacco" and a "Silk" and a "Tea Chest". And then there's a "Nutmeg" and a "Ginger".' My brain was sifting through all the other nameplates on the bedroom doors. 'Although we've also got a "Calico" which I'm pretty sure is some sort of dance music. Oh, yes, and Mum's in "Moonshine" which has got nothing to do with smuggling either—'

'Oh, yes it has, Ottillee!' Finn couldn't help grin. 'Your mum likes a bit of a drink, does she?'

'Moonshine's a *drink?* An alcoholic one?' I gasped when Finn nodded. 'But she told me she chose that room because she liked the idea of falling asleep by the light of the moon—'

'Yeah, maybe she does, Ottillee. And maybe she chose it for another reason too!' An even wider grin. 'Actually, it was the drink that did for Judas Crow in the end. It turns out he killed a man over a bottle of brandy and had to flee Cornwall before he was hung for his crimes.'

'Crikey!' Dragondah was getting more scandalous by the minute. 'No wonder Nanna Nessa was going on about the forces of good and evil, hey? Let's just hope the so-called King of Smugglers never shows his face in this part of the world again.'

'Oh, you don't have to worry about that, Ottillee. Judas Crow was even older than Cowenna. He's sure to be long dead by now.'

Vixen whined dolefully, and I almost joined in to tell you the truth. Such despicable deeds were difficult to imagine, especially in an 'Area of Outstanding Natural Beauty' like Dragondah. Yet bloodthirsty criminals had once lurked behind every blade of grass, it seemed. I mean, honestly, you'd have thought at least *one* law-abiding citizen would have spotted the Crows dragging smuggled booty and dead bodies up the cliffs towards Dragondah Hall, wouldn't you? And then my eyes widened with dismay.

'Oh, no, Finn. That's why there's a tunnel leading from the beach all the way to our house, isn't it? The Crows built it so they could smuggle their stuff into Cornwall without being seen.' And then another dreadful thought occurred to me. 'Cripes, do you think your tramp could be a smuggler too? And that's why he's living in the cave?'

'Well, he's definitely up to something—'

'Yeah, he'll be sneaking stuff into our kitchen pantry and out through our front door, won't he? And what's to stop him? There are no bolts on any of our doors, and Mum's *still* not got round to getting us a dog. Honestly, it will serve her blooming right if the two of us are murdered in our beds—'

'Stop panicking, Ottillee. I'm sure it won't come to that—'

'Humph! It's all right for you, Finn. You haven't got a smugglers' tunnel and a nasty piece of work lurking about at the end of it, have you? And your nan's just *told* us to be careful who we trust round here. I mean, honestly—'

'Okay, okay,' Finn interrupted, his tone soothing. 'If it makes you feel any better, we'll go and have it out with the smuggler — I mean, the tramp — right now. Okay?'

And before I could even nod in agreement, Vixen had set off along the sea path like a furry silver bullet. Soon the fox was so far ahead of us that we lost sight of her. We reached the next headland at last, only for Finn to put on the brakes and utter that rude word he liked beginning with an 's'.

'We're too blooming late, Ottillee!' He pointed down towards the powerful waves surging up the sands. 'There's hardly any beach left as it is. Oh, blast!'

This as he spotted Vixen making her way across the stones at the top of the cove. Another few seconds and the fox had disappeared from view behind the boulder. Finn didn't bother to hide his frustration.

'The daft animal probably thinks Shadow's hiding out in that stupid cave again.' He blew out his cheeks. 'I'll have to go in and fetch her—'

'I'll come with you.'

'No, you stay here. It's far too dangerous.'

'But, Finn, you know the cave doesn't get flooded now. And that there's no dragon in there either—'

'It's not the water *or* the dragon I'm worried about, Ottillee. It's the tramp.'

'But isn't that what we're doing here? To find out what the tramp's up to?'

'Yeah, but it'll be high tide soon, and we don't want to

get *trapped* in a cave with him, do we? What if he *does* turn nasty? Now stay here, Ottillee. I'll be back in a jiffy.'

'But Finn—'

'Stay here, Ottillee.'

'But—'

'I said STAY HERE!'

Finn tossed me such a stern look that I did as I was told. But not for long. And not because I didn't appreciate being bossed around by boys. (Which I most certainly did *not*.) No, it was because Finn had forgotten something. I sneaked down the steps and caught up with him at the entrance to the cave.

'I *told* you to stay on the cliff,' Finn hissed at me angrily.

'And now I'm telling *you* something,' I hissed back. 'You don't have to worry about getting trapped in the cave.'

'But there's hardly any beach left as it is. Another fifteen minutes or so, and we'll be cut off from the steps completely—'

'Yes, but there's another escape route, isn't there?'

'There is?'

'Yes, the secret tunnel, of course!'

'Oh yeah.' A sheepish grin. 'I'd forgotten all about that.'

'Then it's a good job *I'm* here, isn't it?' And before Finn could think of another reason to stop me, I stepped into the cave for the second time that day. 'Now mind your head — this first bit's quite low and narrow.'

And I must admit I was glad of Finn's company as I led him deeper into the darkness. After all, I didn't have Dad's torch lighting the way this time, did I? And not only that, I was secretly starting to wonder whether Finn and I were biting off more than we could chew and heading for real danger here.

I put my finger to my lips as we approached the cavern, listening out for the tramp's coughs and sneezes. But when I peered nervously around the bend, there were no signs of life — no Vixen, no Shadow and certainly no sickly tramp. I glanced at Finn, unsure whether to feel relief or disappointment, but he was far too busy striding forward and gazing all about him.

'Wow, Ottillee, have you ever been anywhere so spooky in your whole life! No wonder Nan didn't want me anywhere near this place.' The eyes that met mine were bright with wonder. 'And where's that strange light coming from? It's almost like a spotlight on a stage, isn't it?'

'Oh, never mind the light, Finn,' I said impatiently as I dragged him over to the pile of belongings. 'What do you make of all this stuff?'

Finn bent down for a closer look. I could tell nothing

had been moved since that morning. The sleeping bag was still rolled up, and the soap, water bottle, toothbrush and Cornish Creamies were right next to it. Then I did notice something.

'Hey, wait a sec. The Dragondah Chronicles are missing.'

'The Dragondah what?'

'The Dragondah *Chronicles*. The book that was here is missing.'

'Yeah, well, maybe the tramp prefers to do his reading outside. And who the heck can blame him, Ottillee?' Finn straightened back up before giving a mock shiver. 'This cave's as cold as the grave, isn't it?'

I nodded, my narrowed eyes on the boulder concealing the entrance to the secret tunnel. I only hoped the tramp *was* outside reading and not roaming about Dragondah Hall with his smuggler's swag bag. I was going to secure that pantry door the first chance I got.

'You okay, Ottillee?' Finn asked as he spotted me shivering for real this time.

'Yeah, of course. I've just got a strange feeling that — oh, I don't know how to describe it — that something *bad's* about to happen.'

Finn took one look at my worried expression. 'Okay, I think we've seen enough for now anyway,' he said firmly as the sound of stones being dragged back down the beach by the incoming tide started to reach our ears. 'The tramp's obviously not here, so let's find Vixen and get back outside again while we still can, okay?'

I nodded gratefully, only to jump out of my skin when Finn started yelling at the top of his voice.

'Vixen, where are you, girl? Shadow's not here, you skogyn, so come back, will you? COME BACK RIGHT NOW!'

But nothing emerged from the shadows and, as I watched Finn continue his search, I felt another shiver run through my body. There's something very odd going on in here, I thought to myself. I knew it in my bones. I could feel it in my water. Finn was inspecting ledges, looking behind boulders, calling Vixen's name over and over again, but she'd vanished into thin air. And how could that have happened? I mean, we'd seen the fox run into the cave with our very own eyes.

Then suddenly, a light bulb went on in my head. Oh, how stupid was I? Why hadn't I thought of it before? Vixen had discovered the secret smuggling tunnel, hadn't she? The clever creature was probably sitting in front of the pantry's little white door, having sniffed out our stinky cheeses and lemon-scented bath bombs. I was just about to call out to Finn when my heart lurched in my chest.

14

'Stranger Danger!'

A MAN WAS walking out of the shadows towards me. To my further shock, Vixen was trotting along by his side, looking for all the world as though she was being taken for a walk by her devoted master. The man came to a halt about ten steps away and put a finger to his lips to stop me from crying out with fright. But he was far too late for that.

'Finn!' I shrieked.

'Bit busy right now, Ottillee!'

Finn's reply came from somewhere behind me, as muffled as it was curt. But my head was screaming 'Stranger Danger!' and I was in no mood to be brushed off.

'*Finn!*' I cried again, looking over my shoulder to see him peering behind a boulder. 'Come *here!*'

'Why? What's going on?' Finn didn't so much as glance in my direction. 'Honestly, Vixen's found herself a cracking hiding place this time. Anyone would think she doesn't *want* to be found.'

I looked back at the fox now sitting contentedly at the man's feet.

'Yeah, you might be right there,' I replied as calmly as I could manage. I was using my sing-songy voice now. The sing-songy voice I used whenever I'd spotted a spider and didn't want it to make any sudden moves. 'Because you know before when you said the tramp wasn't here?'

'Ah-huh?'

'Well, you were wrong!'

As I did my best to alert Finn to the danger, I kept my eyes fixed upon the new arrival. Because I'd never seen anyone like him before in my life. I mean, if Bumstead Billy had always looked like he'd stepped out of a hedge, this man looked like he'd stepped out of a history book. His dark, wild hair had been dragged back into a ponytail. His heavy winter coat had fallen open to reveal black breeches, a baggy white shirt and tall leather boots. And while he can't have been much older than my dad, he certainly wasn't in the best of health. His gaunt face was set off by bloodshot eyes, and his waxy skin clearly hadn't seen the sun in weeks.

And then the man smiled at me and, to my eternal shame, I gasped with shock. Not because it wasn't a nice smile, warm and friendly and a little bit unsure of itself. No, it was because his two very pointed *side* teeth were as unexpected as they were shocking. Then just as the man cleared his throat to say something, Finn dashed up and cut him off.

'Stay away from her, you smuggling — you smuggling dollop of frogspawn, you!' Finn was holding his fists aloft and hopping about from foot to foot like a skinny prize fighter. 'Run, Ottillee, run! It's your last chance!'

'I'm going nowhere, Finn!' I yelled back with my eyes fixed upon the stranger. 'Who knows what he'll do to you!'

And then the stranger *did* do something to Finn. Just not what I'd feared. He held his right hand out towards him, his eyes twinkling with affection.

'You don't know how long I've waited for this moment, Finn,' he rasped in a painfully croaky voice. 'What an honour it is to meet you at last. Well, meet you *properly*, that is.'

'Huh, that's rich, isn't it?' Finn lowered his fists but still ignored the man's outstretched hand. 'I've never met you before in my life. Just seen you skulking about in the distance like a common thief these past few months.'

'Huh! Make your mind up, lad! Common thief or smuggling dollop of frogspawn, which one am I?'

Finn ignored the impossible question, beckoning Vixen towards him instead. But to his clear shock and dismay, the fox simply huddled closer to the man who had now turned his attention to me.

'And may I say what a delight it is to finally meet you too, young Ottillee.'

'What? You know me as well?'

'I know *about* you, child, that's all.' He smiled his unsettling smile. 'You're the new mistress of Dragondah Hall, aren't you?'

'What the heck—?'

The man chuckled at my bewilderment, but it soon turned into a sneezing fit. Then a hacking cough that seemed to go on forever. When Vixen began whining with distress, I knew I had no choice but to put my First Aid training to good use. I patted the man on the back while instructing him to take deep, calming breaths. Finally, the coughing and sneezing stopped.

'Hey, Ottillee, what's going on here?' Finn wasn't impressed by my Girl Guide skills. 'It doesn't take much for *you* to change your mind, does it? One minute the man's about to murder you in your bed, and the next minute he's your patient!'

'Yeah, well, erm—' I was struggling to explain myself. 'It's just that Vixen seems to trust him, doesn't she? And now that I've actually met him, he seems — erm, he seems quite nice.'

I wasn't surprised to find myself on the receiving end of a scowl. 'Quite nice, Ottillee? Quite *nice?* But we don't know a single thing about him!' Finn tapped a side tooth meaningfully. 'Other than he looks like a vam—'

'Finn, no!' I cautioned.

But Finn's scowl was directed at the stranger now. 'So, you, why *are* you hanging around this cave? What have you done to my Vixen? How do you know Ottillee and me? And — and who the heck *are* you?'

The stranger chose not to answer this barrage of questions straight away. Instead, he dropped to his knees and stroked Vixen's head. The fox closed her eyes, and for a long moment, the only sounds that could be heard in the cave were the waves pounding against the rocks outside. One of our escape routes had now been cut off, I realised, and the man seemed to sense my uneasiness. He returned to his feet and met Finn's gaze, his dark eyes glowing with a strange intensity.

'My name's Arlock, Finn, and I've known your family all my life. Your grandfather Tristan was a great character, God rest his soul, and your dad was — well, I like to think Cador was the best friend I ever had.'

I couldn't help gasp, recalling Nanna Nessa's recent pronouncements. That Finn was about to come face to face with his destiny. So, had the old lady *known* this stranger was going to speak to us? Not that Finn's gaze wasn't still full of suspicion.

'My dad's dead,' was all he said, his voice flat with no hint of emotion.

'No need to remind me of that, lad. The day your parents died was the worst of my life.'

'What?' Finn's body jolted, almost as though he'd received an electric shock. 'You knew my mum too?'

'Course I did. Rebecca was the sweetest woman who ever drew breath. Nanna Nessa loved her more like a daughter than the niece she was. Why do you think she took *you* in, lad?'

'You're saying Nan's my — my *aunt?*' Finn stuttered.

'More like your great-*great* aunt, lad. On your mother's side of the family, of course.'

Finn's body stayed statue-still for several seconds. But his face was betraying all sorts of emotions, from pain to confusion, and then his eyes hardened again.

'So tell me this, Arlock, if you know so much about my family, how come I've never met you before? How come I've never even heard your name mentioned?'

Arlock's only reply was a massive sneeze. 'Sorry about that,' he mumbled into a large white hanky. 'I can't seem to shake off this blasted chill. What was your question again?'

Finn rolled his eyes, and I threw him a warning look. I mean, even if *he* wasn't prepared to give Arlock the benefit of the doubt, I certainly was.

'Finn asked why he's never met you before?' I repeated politely, ignoring Finn's snort of derision. Arlock ignored it too.

'Oh, right, yes.' He gave Finn a strange little smile. 'But I think it's best if I answer that question with one of my own. How do you *know* you've never met me before?'

'Huh! I'm sure I wouldn't forget someone who looks like you, Arlock!'

I gasped at Finn's rudeness, but Arlock simply smiled the insult away.

'Don't be too sure, lad. Some people have a clever way of blending into the background when it suits them.'

Finn looked long and hard at Arlock now. As did I. I mean, what the heck did *that* mean? How could someone who looked like Arlock blend into the background? The stranger was being deliberately mysterious, and it was obvious from Finn's tightly clenched jaw that he didn't like it one bit. It was up to me to play peacemaker, I realised.

'Oh, Arlock, forget about Finn for now,' I said. 'Tell me how you know about me? I'm positive I've never met you before. I've only been living in Cornwall a couple of days.'

Arlock's eyes twinkled at me. 'Yes, indeed, young lady, but still long enough to make your presence felt, hey? I'm only surprised you didn't help yourself to one of my Cornish Creamies this morning!'

Cripes! So Arlock had known it was me who'd been nosing through his personal belongings earlier. I didn't know what to say, my red cheeks confirming my guilt. But to my surprise, his smile only grew wider.

'Oh, don't fret, child. You've clearly inherited your father's adventurous spirit.'

'What?' I gasped. 'You know about *my* dad too?'

'Indeed I do. And may I say what an honour it is to have the daughter of such a brave man living here in Dragondah.'

'Thanks, erm, thanks very much,' I mumbled, carefully avoiding Finn's gaze. 'But you still haven't told me how you found out I *was* living here?'

'Let's just say a very well-informed—' Arlock's eyes slid down to the fox at his feet, 'or should I say very *nosy* local alerted me the second you arrived at Dragondah Hall the other day.'

'Oh, yes, of course! I remember seeing Vixen run off into the trees when we drove up.'

'Yes, she's been waiting months for your arrival, Ottillee. As have we all.' Arlock's eyes were twinkling again. 'And you're most welcome here, child. I know you won't let us down.'

'Let — let you *down?*' I shot a puzzled glance at Finn. 'What do you mean?'

But Finn had clearly had enough of our conversation. 'Honestly, Ottillee, you're not falling for any of this guff, are you?' he scoffed. 'The man's just buttering you up. Getting you on his side, like he's done with my Vixen. He's probably why Shadow keeps flying off too.'

I started to protest, but Finn was in no mood to listen and turned his frustration on Arlock.

'Yes, you! Why *do* you keep luring my animals into this cave?' he demanded, his hands balled into fists. 'Making them forget where their *real* home is? In fact, now I come to think about it, it'll be you who's given Shadow his cold. And now he's gone missing again. If you've hurt him, I'll—'

'Oh honestly, lad, what do you take me for?' Arlock stifled another sneeze.

'Do you *really* want me to answer that?'

'Finn!' I chided. I'd no idea where all his anger was coming from. I mean, this was more than an understandable wariness of some cave-dwelling stranger. This was open hostility.

'Well, where *is* Shadow, Ottillee?' Finn's expression was bordering on desperate now. 'Why's he flying away from me first chance he gets? For all I know, he could be the other side of Cornwall by now.'

But it was Arlock who placed a reassuring hand on Finn's shoulder. 'Do try not to worry, lad,' he said soothingly. 'He's not far away, I promise. And he'll be back by your side before you know it.'

'Oh, so you *do* know where he is!' Finn knocked Arlock's hand away. 'And you'd better be telling the truth. Because if you've damaged one hair on his head, you'll live to rue the day!'

'Oh my! Not just your father's eyes, but his temper too!'

Arlock's chesty chuckle only irritated Finn further.

'I'm off,' he snapped, but I held him back.

'But Finn, don't you want to know what's going on?' Without waiting for a reply, I turned back to Arlock. 'Will you *please* just tell us exactly what you're doing here? You know, to put our minds at rest.'

Finn and I waited for what seemed like an eternity for a response. And when Arlock finally replied, all traces of his earlier amusement had vanished. His eyes were flinty, and his voice was unwavering.

'I'm here to help you save Dragondah.'

'Blithering barnacles!' Finn was exasperated.

'Save Dragondah from *what?*' I was intrigued.

Arlock considered us for another few seconds, his gaunt face giving nothing away.

'Follow me,' was all he said.

———◦◇◦———

'The Rainbow?'

IN THE HALF-LIGHT of the cavern, I looked at Finn, and Finn looked at me. Then we both looked at Arlock.

'Follow you *where?*' Finn demanded, still making no effort to hide his mistrust.

'You'll see soon enough, lad.'

'Hey, Arlock, we're not moving a muscle until we know *exactly* where you're taking us.'

'Oh, Finn, let's just do what—'

But Arlock raised a hand to silence me. 'No, Ottillee, it's a reasonable enough request,' he rasped, his eyes still fixed upon Finn. 'We're going to Dragondah Peek.'

'Oh, who do you think *you're* kidding?' Finn scoffed. 'There are no mountain peaks in Dragondah. And I should know. I've lived here all my life.'

'You're right, of course.' Arlock continued to overlook Finn's disrespect. 'But Dragondah Peek's got nothing to do with mountains, lad. Now follow me — if you know what's good for you.'

Arlock turned on his heels, and Vixen darted off after him. After a brief hesitation, I made as if to do the same.

'Where the heck are *you* going?' Finn grabbed my arm, his voice a loud whisper.

'I'm going after Arlock,' I whispered back.

'But what if he's leading us into danger? Don't forget it's high tide out there now.' Finn's eyes were pleading as they met mine. 'Come on, let's make a run for it along your tunnel.'

'But, Finn—' I glanced over my shoulder at the disappearing figures, 'if Vixen's following Arlock, don't you think we should too?'

'Oh, Arlock's bewitched Vixen.' Finn was now looking truly anguished. 'You too, by the look of it. Pretending he knew who you were and all that rubbish.'

'But he *does* know who I am, Finn. And he definitely knows who you are. He knows your nan too. And he knows all about your grandfather and your dad and even your mum—'

'Huh! That's if any of it's even true, Ottillee. Nan would never keep important stuff like that from me.'

She would if she thought she was protecting you, I wanted to say, recalling Nanna Nessa's recent admissions. But knowing this would only unsettle Finn further, what I *actually* said was, 'Honestly, Finn, anyone would think you were scared of Arlock! Now come on. Let's get after him, and find out what the heck's going on!'

I knew Finn wouldn't be able to resist such a challenge, and I was right. Although even *my* resolve faltered as we neared the cave's exit and could hear the waves smashing against the cliffs outside. Then just as Finn swore under his breath and I gave an urgent little cough, Arlock surprised us by leading Vixen *away* from the beach to the right. And it wasn't long before the four of us were climbing higher with every step we took, some unknown hand having chiselled a rough stairway deep inside the rock.

A chesty Arlock was soon finding it difficult to put one foot in front of the other, his breathing laboured and his movements increasingly unsteady. And I wasn't the only one concerned he might collapse at any moment. Vixen kept glancing over her shoulder as if begging Finn and me to insist on a break.

'I *really* don't think I can go on much longer,' I finally panted as we rounded a sharp bend. I was clutching dramatically at my chest and breathing even harder than Arlock was. 'Because my heart's about to—'

And then I was stunned into silence. Arlock and Vixen had finally come to a halt at a large opening in the cliff face. The pair of them were silhouetted against a vast expanse of sky, a sky still so full of clouds that it was a pure and dazzling white.

'It gives me great pleasure to welcome you to Dragondah Peek!' Arlock just about managed a mock flourish as we joined him as close to the edge of the cliff as we dared. 'Aptly titled, I think you'll both agree? Oh yes, and I don't need to warn you to watch your step, do I?'

'No, you *don't!*' I took my courage in both hands and peeked over the edge of the precipice. 'Oh, dithering doodahs!'

'Blithering barnacles, more like!'

Finn was as taken aback as I was by the staggering views spread out in front of us. The sweeping arc of Dragondah Bay was visible for miles. We were so high up that a couple of birds, a feisty seagull and an even feistier crow, were wrangling over scraps of food far beneath us. But even more jaw-dropping was what was directly in front of us.

Dragondah Castle, which I knew to be far out on an island in the middle of the bay, suddenly seemed so close that I was tempted to reach out my hand and touch it. Who knew that its stone walls were so thick? That its windows were nothing more than narrow cracks? And that at the top of the tower, there was a wooden door with two dragon-shaped hinges?

Then, just as a ray of sunlight pierced the clouds and a rainbow formed across the bay, I realised that what I'd been seeing with so much clarity had simply been a trick of the light. That the castle was nowhere near touching distance, and that there was still a wide stretch of water swelling and dipping between us.

'Still think this place is boring, Ottillee?'

'Oh, but I never—' I turned to see Arlock's knowing gaze on my face. Cripes! Could this strange man read minds too? 'Well, yes, I didn't think much of Dragondah *at first*, I'll admit. It was just so different from back home in Bumstead, you see—'

'Yes, but you've got a *new* home now, haven't you, child? And I can see that you already appreciate Dragondah's unique place in the world.' He grinned at me, his breathing almost back to normal. 'You're one of us now, young lady, whether you like it or not!'

I found myself smiling at Arlock's heart-warming words. But my smile soon faded.

'Well, this is all very touching, isn't it?' Finn scoffed. 'Getting a bit side-tracked though, aren't we, Arlock? You dragged us all the way up here to tell us something important, so just get on with it, will you?'

'Always in a rush, exactly like your dad!'

Finn's expression turned thunderous. 'Okay, Ottillee, let's get going. This is nothing but a wild goose chase, this is. There's nothing to see here.'

But Arlock's next words stopped Finn in his tracks. 'Well, I'd have thought that even *you* could see that,' he said, his bony finger pointing out to sea.

'Dragondah Castle?' Finn sighed. 'So what, Arlock? I've seen that castle a million times.'

'But have you ever seen *that*, Finn?'

'The rainbow?'

'No!'

'That grey seal bobbing about out there?'

'*Seal?*' I scanned the sea excitedly, but with no luck.

'No, not the seal! Look at the castle's eastern wall between those two windows. Or arrow slits to give them their proper name.' Arlock's finger stabbed the air. 'Concentrate hard, the pair of you — don't you see anything yet?'

'All I can see is the same old ruin I've always seen,' Finn retorted. 'Oh, what a waste of time this is. Come on, Ottillee, let's get out of here.'

But I was concentrating so hard that I didn't respond. I narrowed my eyes and swept them from the top to the bottom of the castle wall, and then from the bottom to the top. I repeated this several times without noticing anything remarkable. Then just as I was about to give up, the wall suddenly came into sharp focus. Hardly able to believe what I was seeing, I gasped and grabbed Finn's arm.

'Look, Finn!' I cried. 'Start at the top of the wall and work your way down. A man's face is carved into the stone — clear as day, it is!'

Finn released a heavy sigh. 'I can't see a blasted thing.'

'Then look again, you skogyn! See, the man's got one eye open and one eye shut. And there's his nose, and his mouth, and his chin. With a big — you know, *groove* in it like yours.' I stared at Finn for a long moment and then back at the wall. 'Actually, the man looks exactly like you!'

Finn looked again. This time his gaze narrowed. And was that a gasp of recognition? But if he was impressed by what he saw, he refused to show it.

'Oh, right, I see it. So what?'

'I'll give you "so what", lad.' Arlock finally lost his temper. He stepped towards Finn, his eyes glinting with anger. 'That's the face of the great King Locryn Penhaligon, that is. That's the face of the man who reigned over a golden period in Cornish history. A period of great peace and culture. A period when goodness finally triumphed over evil—'

'But—'

'No, Finn, listen to me now.' Arlock was pointing at the castle again. 'A master craftsman carved King Locryn's likeness into that wall a thousand years ago. And, despite Cornwall's raging winter storms, it's just about withstood the test of time.'

'Yeah, well, who cares about something that happened a thousand years ago?'

'*You* should care, lad. Because even you must be able to see you look exactly like your illustrious ancestor.'

'My — my *ancestor?*'

'Yes, lad, you've got the same cleft in the chin as the young King Locryn, the same wide mouth and, most important of all, the same remarkable eyes, one of them blue and one of them green—'

'Oh, what poppycock, Arlock!' Now it was Finn's turn to stab his finger in the air. 'Who the heck *knows* what colour those eyes are? They're carved in stone, they are. And one of them's even closed!'

'Yes, lad, but that's how the king's eyes were always depicted in medieval times. One of them open and one of them closed to mark, no *celebrate* their different colours. A characteristic very few people in this world are blessed with—'

'Although my—'

'What was that, Ottillee?'

My gaze dropped to the ground. 'Oh, erm, nothing.'

The last thing Arlock needed was for me to reveal that my dad had different-coloured eyes too. Because then Finn would *never* believe he was related to King Locryn.

'Yes, lad, there's no doubt about it,' Arlock continued. 'You're a Penhaligon, a Penhaligon through and through.'

'You're deluded, Arlock! I'm no Penhaligon!'

Finn's expression was so desperate that my heart went out to him. I winced when Vixen trotted up to nuzzle his leg, only to be totally ignored.

'What *is* your last name then?' I asked Finn softly.

'I don't have one,' he ground out, flinching as a large bird flew past his head with a shrill squawk. 'I thought you understood that, Ottillee? Finn's enough of a name for me. Always has been, always will.'

'Yeah, but everyone's got a last name, Finn. I mean, that's just how the world works. My last name's Bottomly and I'm proud of it. *Really* proud of it actually because I got it from my dad.'

'Exactly!' Arlock grabbed Finn's shoulders so roughly that Vixen scampered out of the way. 'And you should be really proud of your last name too, lad. Because you got it from Cornwall's greatest ever king. Like it or not, Finn Penhaligon, *you* are King Locryn's last living descendant.'

And with this, Arlock was overcome by a coughing fit and forced to let Finn go. Finn just stared at him soundlessly, clearly in shock. And who could blame him? I mean, yes, Nanna Nessa had already told me that she'd shielded her boy from some important truths, but these were more like lightning bolts, weren't they? I just knew the old lady would want me to help Finn make sense of it all.

'So, are you saying what I *think* you're saying?' I asked Arlock when he'd finally recovered enough to speak.

'And what's that, Ottillee?'

'That Finn is, erm, the King of Cornwall?'

16

'A Penhaligon Princess?'

I COULD HARDLY believe I'd asked Arlock such a ridiculous question. Was Finn the King of Cornwall indeed? But even *more* ridiculous was that Arlock was actually nodding at me!

'Yes, Ottillee, if history had taken a different path, that petulant young man over there would have been crowned the King of Cornwall.'

'Crikey! Did you hear that, Finn?'

I swung round, only to see Finn gazing out to sea as if this astonishing announcement had nothing to do with him. Honestly, what was the matter with the boy? I was literally bursting with questions.

'So, why isn't Finn living in Dragondah Castle then?' was my first one.

'Oh, that's rather hard to explain—'

'Can't you at least *try?*'

Arlock sighed. 'Well, I suppose the main reason is that

the Cornish throne no longer exists. Not officially anyway. When Cornwall was swallowed up by England many centuries ago, the Penhaligons simply went to ground.'

'Went to *ground?* What do you mean?'

'I mean they blended in with their surroundings, Ottillee. In fact, most of King Locryn's descendants, certainly his *heirs*, became travellers. They lived like Finn's living to this very day.'

Once again, I tried to gauge Finn's reaction to these revelations, but his attention remained fixed upon the view. The rainbow had faded now, the castle once more backdropped by grey skies. Again I had the feeling that it had long given up hope of anyone coming to its rescue.

'But how could the Penhaligons abandon their family *home* like that?' I asked, only for Arlock to address his reply to Finn. Or rather to Finn's back.

'What if I told you that they hadn't abandoned it, lad? That over the centuries, your family had done their best to maintain their castle. Your grandfather even added some rather basic bathroom facilities. Other interested parties—' a sniff here, 'have done their best to keep King Locryn's bedchamber in order.'

No response from Finn, yet *still* Arlock persisted.

'Yes, you were born in that bedchamber, Finn Penhaligon. As is tradition for the heir to the long-lost Cornish throne.' A hesitation now, as though Arlock was weighing his next words carefully. 'And as is *also* tradition, Dragondah Castle is now your responsibility, young man.'

Still no reaction from Finn, but a wide-eyed 'Cripes!' from me.

'Yes, Ottillee, and you'd better brace yourself for another shock.' Arlock swung round to face *me* now. 'Because it's your solemn duty to help Finn.'

'My solemn *duty?*' I challenged. 'But what are you talking about? I mean, I'll help Finn, of course I will, but what's any of this got to do with me?'

'Well, wasn't it *you* who Cowenna chose to take over her estate?'

'So?'

'So Cowenna was also a member of the Cornish royal family.' Arlock smiled as my eyes almost popped out of my head. 'Yes, Ottillee, your benefactress might have died a lonely Crow widow, but she was born a beloved Penhaligon princess.'

'A Penhaligon prin — princess?' I stuttered, my mind racing. 'But that makes no sense at all. Why would a Cornish princess leave everything she owned to a London schoolgirl like me? I mean, I didn't even *know* her!'

I waited for the answer with bated breath. My heart was pounding. My throat was dry. Arlock was about to solve the mystery behind my strange legacy. But much to my dismay, he was shaking his head.

'Sorry, child, I'm as clueless about your inheritance as you are. All *I* know is that Cowenna was a canny one who never left anything to chance.'

I released a frustrated sigh, only for Arlock to smile at me wryly.

'Yes, maybe there'll be some sort of clue in the family archives, hey?' He wiped his nose with his hanky. 'Although who knows where The Dragondah Chronicles are hiding? And believe me, I've not left a stone unturned these past ten years.'

'But Arlock, I saw The Dragondah Chronicles only this morning!' I gasped. 'You know, with all your other stuff. I'm really sorry, I didn't know everything belonged to you.'

'Oh, don't you worry, child. And anyway, this rubbish isn't worth the paper it's printed on.' To my astonishment, Arlock pulled the book out of his coat pocket and tossed it carelessly over the edge of the cliff. We could hear it clattering down the rocks before splashing into the sea. 'One of the Penhaligons will have put those blank pages together to mislead their enemies. Cador's the most likely candidate, to my mind. Finn's dad always fancied himself a bit of a joker!'

For some reason, these words finally woke Finn from his trance. 'So The Dragondah Chronicles — I mean, the *real* Dragondah Chronicles are important, are they?'

Finn's response was still empty of any real emotion, but

Arlock took it as an encouraging sign.

'Yes, they're very important, lad. The Chronicles are a written history of the Cornish royal family, many of the pages penned by King Locryn Penhaligon himself. They're a record of births, deaths and everything in between. And even more crucially, they include written proof, legal proof if you like, of everything they — well, *you* — still own.'

'Humph! That can't be much!'

Finn's voice was full of scorn, and Arlock's eyes narrowed on him.

'So gold coins and rare jewels aren't *much* then, hey?'

'Gold coins and rare jewels?'

'Yes, lad, they're all part of King Locryn's missing fortune. And, believe me, you'll be needing as much money as you can get your hands on if you're going to take over Dragondah Castle—'

'Take it *over?*'

'Yes, Finn, haven't you been listening to a word I've said? You *own* that magnificent pile of stone out there! You just need the castle deeds — or rather The Dragondah Chronicles — to prove it!'

A moment of stunned silence from both Finn *and* me this time. Then Finn gave a weary shake of his head as if it was all too much for him. Again, it was up to me to try and make sense of it all.

'Well, if Finn *is* King Locryn's heir—' I could hardly

believe I was saying such a thing out loud, 'who the heck lost these Dragondah Chronicles in the first place? I hope they've got a really good excuse because, honestly—'

'Yes, they *have* got a really good excuse, Ottillee.'

'So what is it?'

'They're dead.'

My hands flew to my mouth. 'Oops, sorry—'

'Yes, only the heirs to the Cornish throne know where The Dragondah Chronicles are hidden.' Arlock coughed into his hanky before meeting Finn's wide-eyed gaze. 'Your father Cador was their last custodian, lad. Had he not died well before his time, he'd have revealed their whereabouts to you on the day you turned sixteen, just as royal tradition dictates—'

'On the day I turned *sixteen?*'

'Yes, he'd have brought you up to Dragondah Peek. He'd have shown you King Locryn's face in the stone, and he'd have told you all about your royal heritage. Exactly like I did today—'

'Then you had no right to do that, did you?' Finn snarled. 'Even if any of this is true, you're not my father, are you? And I'm nowhere near sixteen yet—'

'Finn! Just *listen* to Arlock, will you?' I urged. 'He's only trying to help you.'

Arlock smiled his thanks at me before turning back to Finn.

'Everything you said just now is true, lad. But royal tradition went out of the window the second your father died and took the whereabouts of The Dragondah Chronicles with him. I *had* to tell you who you are today because — because—'

'Because *what?*' Finn and I echoed.

'Because dark forces are circling Dragondah again.'

'Oh, no, not you too!' I couldn't help cry. I mean, what was it with the grown-ups round here? Anyone would think Dragondah was still awash with dangerous wreckers and smugglers! And just as Nanna Nessa had done earlier, Arlock failed to back up his dramatic claim.

'Yes, sorry, Ottillee. Take no notice of an old prophet of doom like me. You youngsters just concentrate on what I'm asking you to do over these coming weeks. That's a heavy enough burden as it is.'

'But what *are* you asking us to do?' Finn and I chorused.

'I'm asking you to help me find The Dragondah Chronicles before it's too late.'

And on dropping this final bombshell, Arlock turned on his heels and vanished down the slope. Vixen raced after him, leaving Finn and me to follow in what I can only describe as a dazed silence. By the time we got outside, the tide had receded just enough for us to reach the steps back up the cliff. But somehow, we'd lost Arlock along the way. Only Vixen was waiting for us on the stones, her expression an almost comical mix of innocence and guilt.

'Arlock, where *are* you?' I yelled, my voice echoing eerily back through the cave. 'You've got to help us! We haven't a clue where to start looking for The Dragondah Chronicles!'

We waited and waited, but the only one to finally respond to my calls was Shadow. The bat came soaring out of the cave before landing on Finn's shoulder. He didn't get a good reception.

'Oh, had enough of Arlock for the time being, have you?'

Finn's anger towards Shadow dismayed me, especially as Vixen was getting the same cold treatment. I watched as the trio set off for the stairway, desperately hoping they'd make up soon. Surely Arlock couldn't have destroyed such lifelong friendships in a few hours, could he?

'So what are we going to do?' I shouted after Finn. 'Shall I come to yours so we can put a plan of action together—?'

But my words trailed off. Finn was climbing the steps and didn't so much as glance in my direction. I was left with little choice but to return to Dragondah Hall alone. Alone and troubled. Because Nanna Nessa's strange predictions had come true, hadn't they? Finn *had* come face to face with his destiny today. Inheriting Dragondah Castle *did* mean that his carefree childhood was over. And as for my own inheritance? Well, thanks to Arlock, that little mystery had now taken on a whole new meaning, hadn't it?

Dad's Secret Report

DATE: Monday, 13 August, 2018   TIME: 5am

PLACE: The usual   SUBJECT: Loads of stuff

Dear Dad,

What a nightmare I've just had. But, don't worry, it wasn't about you being swept down a raging river this time. No, this time, I was all alone in the cold and the dark, and I was being chased by — well, I can't actually remember now, Dad, but it was scary enough to wake me up!

And it's no wonder I'm in a bit of a state because you won't believe what I've just found out. Some of it from Nanna Nessa and some of it from a strange man who lives in that cave I told you about. But you don't have to worry, because Arlock's <u>good</u> strange, not bad strange. (Well, Finn's not totally convinced yet, but I'm pretty sure Nanna Nessa knows him. And the fox loves him, so that's good enough for me.) Anyway, whoever said Dragondah was boring (me!) was wrong?!!!

1) First thing you're not going to believe is Dragondah Hall was once the wickedest place in all of Cornwall! It was built by a family of local baddies called the Crows. I know, I was upset at first too. It's not nice to think you're sitting on the same toilet as a smuggler, is it? Or that a wrecker once dragged a dead body through your kitchen. Or that your bedrooms are named after smuggled booty. 'Silk', 'Nutmeg' and 'Calico'*, for example. Anyway, if all this dodgy stuff hadn't happened hundreds of years ago, it would have put me right off my new home. But as Finn said, Dragondah Hall's got itself a <u>new</u> mistress now. And I've no intention of sneaking stuff into the country illegally, no matter how delicious it tastes. And I'm also totally against murdering people, even if I do like the look of their jewellery.

2) I've also discovered some TRULY AMAZING stuff about Finn and Dragondah Castle. Turns out the castle's the home of the Cornish royal family!!! But the Penhaligons were forced into hiding (well, horseboxes) many centuries ago. Finn's the last of the Penhaligons and so the castle's real owner. Ace news, yes? But no, Finn can't stake his claim because he's got zero proof. The castle deeds are in something called THE DRAGONDAH CHRONICLES which are LOST!!!! Arlock wants us to help him track them down (they might even lead us to some family treasure!!), but unfortunately, they could be <u>anywhere</u> in Dragondah!!!!

3) Anyway, what's all this got to do with me, I hear you ask? Well, Mrs Crow was Cornish royalty too, if you can believe it? Turns out my

benefactress was a Penhaligon princess abandoned by her family when she married the smuggler, Judas Crow. So now I know why Mrs Crow didn't leave Dragondah Hall to any of her Penhaligon relatives (not even Finn), but I <u>still</u> don't know why she left it to ME!!??!!!! Nanna Nessa said she was sure to have had a <u>good and proper reason.</u> Arlock also insisted Mrs Crow <u>never</u> left anything to chance. We're just hoping the answer <u>also</u> lies in these DRAGONDAH CHRONICLES!!?!!

4) So now the race is on to find these precious archives, Dad. Problem is, time is NOT on our side. And I'm not even joking. I mean, Arlock's already been looking for them for ten years, and I'm starting at my new boarding school in three weeks!! Of course, it doesn't help that Finn's been AWOL for four whole days now!!!? Nanna Nessa told me he was in a 'bit of a strop' and would be back soon, but I'm not so sure. I mean, she's been keeping lots of important family secrets from him, and he did seem pretty upset/shell-shocked the last time I saw him. He didn't even take Vixen or Shadow with him when he left.

5) Finally, Mum's in my bad books again too. Can you believe she's been taking advantage of Finn's absence <u>and</u> the bad weather? She's not only made me bake loads of fairy cakes but she's also made me dust and de-spider every room in the house. (I'm exactly like a Tudor wench forced to do back-breaking manual labour.) I mean, why can't Mum <u>finally</u> pick up her new paintbrushes and stop looking for things for ME to do? Or better still, why can't she get us a <u>dog</u>?!!!

Also, Mum recently entertained a friend (a man) in the kitchen, and there was lots of inappropriate gossiping, laughing and coffee drinking. And even though I'm desperate to talk this stuff over with someone, I'm not going to talk it over with her. Specially not the Cowenna Crow stuff. Or the Penhaligon stuff. Or The Dragondah Chronicles stuff. I'm scared she'll blab about it to her new friend.

Anyway, Dad, you're all up-to-date now. I could probably think of more stuff to tell you if I wasn't so exhausted due to all the baking, dusting, de-spidering and worry of having to save a Cornish castle ALL BY MYSELF.

Lots of love, as always. Mwah, mwah, mwah!
Your daughter,
Ottillee xxxoooxx

PS: Yes, Dad, I do know I should always tell Mum everything that's going on in my life. And I would, honestly I would, but you haven't met her new friend, have you? Lucifer Branson's a shifty stinker, and I get the feeling he's going to be popping in for coffee and a gossip every chance he gets. I DON'T TRUST HIM ONE LITTLE BIT!!??!!!

PPS: One good thing is my Cornish is coming along well. I can now count to ten (onan, dew, tri, peswar, pymp, hwegh, seyth, eth, naw, deg) and have mastered useful local phrases like 'Giss on!' (you're having a laugh?), and 'Piddledowndidda' (Was it raining?)

PPPS: Oh yes, and you'll be pleased to know my eczema is ALSO tons better thanks to some smelly lime green ointment given to me by Nanna Nessa. Yippee!!

PPPPS: Oh yes, I forgot to tell you. There are <u>seals</u> living in the waters off Dragondah. Yes, actual real-life SEALS!!! Who knows, maybe I'll get to see one close-up one day!!!

* As for 'calico', Dad, don't make the same stupid mistake I did and confuse it with 'calypso'! One's a heavy material and the other one's a type of music. I should have known the Crows weren't much into singing and dancing!

18

'A Bit Of A Wander About?'

'PSSST!'

I was alone in the kitchen finishing my breakfast when I heard a strange hissing sound outside. I'd just opened the window to let the smell of Mum's burnt toast waft over the Dragondah countryside.

'Pssssssssssssssssst!'

There it was again, only this time loud enough to set off the speckled crow. (I was seriously thinking of promoting him to speckled *guard* crow.) I went over to open the back door, only to gasp with relief. Finn was no longer AWOL. He was standing right in front of me wearing his thin blue anorak and a sheepish grin.

'*Whu-de-eck-ov-u-bin?*' I crammed the remainder of my banana-on-toast into my mouth and dragged him inside. '*I-bin-whurd-shick-bowt-u-I-av.*'

Finn waited until I'd swallowed. 'What was that?' he asked, looking me up and down, and grinning even wider.

'I asked where you've *been,* you skogyn*?* I've been worried sick about you! Nanna Nessa said she hadn't seen you in days.'

'Oh, right, yeah, sorry.' Finn shrugged off his anorak and sat down at the table, his eyes darting all about him. 'I just went for a bit of a wander about, that's all. Crikey, this kitchen is enormous!'

'Never mind the kitchen, Finn.' I plonked myself down opposite him. 'What do you mean you went for a bit of a *wander about?* All by yourself? In the rain? For *four* whole days?'

'Yeah, what's wrong with that, Ottillee? I'm used to being by myself, aren't I? And a spot of rain never bothered me. As for sleeping under the stars, I love it, I do.'

Finn treated himself to some of my orange juice before treating me to yet another stupid grin. Although this time, it was more of a smirk, and I released a heavy sigh. Because something wasn't quite right here. I mean, yes, Finn was back to his usual irritating self, but was it normal to be your usual irritating self when you'd just had some life-changing news? Finn was acting like the events at Dragondah Peek had never even happened.

'So why didn't you take Vixen and Shadow with you on this "bit of a wander about"?' I asked, almost jumping out of my skin when he slammed the glass of orange juice down on the table.

'Huh! Couldn't get away from those two fast enough, I couldn't. Nan too, come to think of it. Traitors, the whole bunch of them.'

Traitors, hey? I mean, yes, I was pleased Finn had finally stopped grinning like an idiot, but that was a bit over the top, wasn't it?

'So you told your nan what Arlock said to you, did you?' I asked, careful to move the drink out of his reach first. 'That she's not really your grandmother but your—'

'Yeah, I told her.'

'And how you're King Locryn's heir?'

'Yeah, of course I told her about that. But it turns out that Nan's known I'm a Penhaligon all along. *And* she knows Arlock as well. From years back, she admitted.'

'Oh, right.' I wasn't going to admit I'd suspected that.

'Yeah, Arlock showed up in Dragondah again back in the spring, she said.' Finn sighed heavily. 'He wanted to tell me who I was then, but Nan made him keep out of my way. She wouldn't let him speak to me until *you* got here.'

'Crikey.' Even *I'd* not expected that. 'But how did your nan even *know* about me back in the spring?'

'Oh, yeah, Nan lied about that too.' A tightening of Finn's lips. 'She didn't find out you'd inherited Dragondah Hall from me last week. Doctor Denzel told her all about you back in April. Turns out he's a friend of Cowenna Crow's solicitor over in Bodmin.'

I nodded slowly, quite taken aback by all these grown-up shenanigans. Although it did explain a few things, and unlike Finn, I decided to give both Arlock and Nanna Nessa the benefit of the doubt.

'Yeah, well, I'm sure everyone was just trying to do their best by you, Finn,' I said. 'Discovering you're the heir to the Cornish throne is quite a big thing, you know, especially when you're only eleven. Maybe Nanna Nessa just wanted you to have some support from someone your own age—'

'Pfft! I can look after myself well enough, Ottillee. I was born and bred round these parts, wasn't I? Can you believe Nan didn't even think I'd go up Dragondah Peek without you?'

I didn't like to point out that Finn *wouldn't* have gone up Dragondah Peek without me. He wouldn't even have stepped inside the cave without me. So, I just let him drink his juice and calm down. Finally, he glanced at me from under his brows.

'Anyway, Ottillee, I still don't believe a word of all this king stuff, do you? It's total rubbish, isn't it?'

'Yes, your majesty.'

Finn didn't even crack a smile, and I frowned. Mmmm, things still weren't right here. My friend was clearly 'in denial' about his new royal status. (Just as I was 'in denial' about Dad's death, according to my old counsellor back in London.) Anyway, I was the last person in the world to offer advice, so I settled for asking Finn a few questions instead. And once I'd got started, I could hardly stop.

Did Finn really not think he was of royal birth? Did Finn really not think he was the spitting image of King Locryn? But most important of all, did Finn really not think we should at least *start* looking for The Dragondah Chronicles?

And, to give him his due, Finn responded to all my questions with either a nod or a shrug. The annoying smirk was hovering about his mouth again. Then things took another turn when Mum walked in with *The Cornish Clarion* newspaper in her hand.

'Ooooh, you must be Ottillee's new friend Finn!' she gushed, her face lit by a bright smile.

'That's right, Mrs Bottomly.' Finn got to his feet and held out his hand. 'I'm very pleased to meet you.'

'And I'm very pleased to *finally* meet you, young man.' Mum's smile widened even further when she shook Finn's hand and met his gaze. 'Oh, my giddy aunt! You've got — what's the matter, Ottillee?'

This as I was mouthing 'no' and waving my arms about behind Finn's head. The last thing I wanted was for Mum to tell Finn he had the same eyes as my dad. Because if a Bottomly could have different-coloured eyes, then Finn really *would* start questioning his Penhaligon heritage. But, as it happened, Mum had other things on her mind.

'Anyway, Ottillee, I *told* you Lucifer was a decent and honourable man,' she said, referring to the front page of her newspaper. 'Now listen to this—'

'Oh, who cares about that horrible man?'

But Mum ignored me and started reading. '*Millionaire philanthropist Lucifer Branson has just been granted planning permission to develop the long-abandoned Dragondah Castle into a residential home for orphans. The council is confident 'The Dragondah Castle Academy' won't just benefit Cornwall's disadvantaged youngsters but will also breathe new life into this sleepy enclave on our north coast—*'

Mum paused as if she was waiting for me to make a snarky comment, but when my only response was a worried glance at Finn, she carried on.

'*Dragondah has been off the map for years, of course, its royal history lost in the mists of time. Yet rumours are already starting to circulate. Was this scenic hideaway really named after dragonflies? Or is the legend true, and a fearsome dragon once threatened its secluded bays? Secluded bays, moreover, that were also once terrorised by the most infamous wreckers and smugglers in Cornish history—*'

Mum met my narrowed gaze again. 'Gosh, Ottillee, who knew all this was going on in our new home? It's so thrilling, isn't it?'

When all I could manage was a tightening of my lips, she rolled her eyes at me and resumed reading.

'"Dragondah Castle has finally got itself a new and worthwhile purpose," said Lucifer Branson at yesterday's press launch at the Chuggypig Inn. "The lucky kids will not only live and learn on-site but they'll also be encouraged to make the most of the breathtaking coastal scenery. And although I was neither born nor bred in Cornwall, I've assured the council that the local wildlife will be protected, and the castle's history will be given all the respect it deserves."'

Mum scowled at my heavy sigh before carrying on.

'Indeed, the children could hardly have a better role model than this modest businessman who prefers to keep his other commercial and philanthropic ventures tightly under wraps. It was only after much pressing that Mr Branson would reveal how he was unfortunate enough to lose his left eye. He was hit by a plank of wood when rescuing his elderly father from a burning building.'

'You're kidding me?'

'Spaces at The Dragondah Castle Academy are limited, of course, and preference will be given to youngsters born in the local area.'

Mum finally put her newspaper down and met my gaze. Hers was steady while mine was — well, confused. I mean, had I made a massive mistake? Was Lucifer Branson not a shifty stinker, after all? Although even if he *wasn't* as bad as I thought he was, he was still taking over someone else's family home without their permission, wasn't he? I mean, talk about the worst timing in the world. Just when Finn discovers *he's* the rightful owner of Dragondah Castle, the council hands it on a plate to some passing philatelist — I mean, philap — I mean *do-gooder.*

And what the heck was Arlock going to say when he found out about it? Surely the only person with the right to turn the Penhaligons' home into a children's home was Finn Penhaligon himself? My dismay must have shown on my face.

'Oh, Ottillee, really.' Mum tutted with annoyance before turning to Finn. 'Take no notice of Miss Grumpy-Knickers over there. Surely *you* can see Lucifer Branson is quite the hero.'

'Well—'

Finn was just about to explain our dilemma when I kicked him under the table.

'Actually, Mum, Finn's in a bit of a rush today. He wants me to help him with some — erm, well, it's *family* stuff really. It's okay if I go out with him, isn't it?'

Mum's gaze flickered over me. 'No, Ottillee, it's not okay.'

'But I've hardly been out for days.'

She shook her head.

'And I've had my brekkie—'

'I am *not* letting you go outside, Ottillee.'

'Why not?' My eyes narrowed. 'Are you still mad at me? Because I know I missed that spider in your wellies. And I know I was wrong about Lucifer Branson being shifty—'

'Oh, Ottillee, it's got nothing to do with the welly spider or Lucifer's shiftiness. We're not *all* sulky schoolgirls like you, you know.'

Mum followed this superior remark with a superior smile which wound me up even further.

'Oh, Mum, this is *so* not fair!' I cried, all the frustrations of the past few days, indeed months, indeed *years*, getting the better of me. 'You drag me to this new place, and then you won't let me spend time with my new friend—'

'Of course I will—'

'And you force me to do all the de-spidering.'

'But I've been doing the sorting out—'

'And there's still no sign of a blinking dog.'

'Oh, give me a chance—'

'And then you let that — that *phil-at-elist* into our house.'

'Oh, honestly, Ottillee, Lucifer's a *philanthropist*—'

'And you give him a coffee out of Dad's footy mug.'

'But Lucifer took the mug before I could stop him—'

'And you told him—' I hesitated, not wanting Finn to know that Mum had been gossiping about him, 'all sorts of *personal* stuff.'

'Honestly, Ottillee, now you're being a drama queen.'

'Oh, a drama queen, am I?' I banged my hand on the table. 'I'll bet no one ever calls *Finn* a drama queen—'

'Drama *king*, I'm thinking?'

'Whatever.' My eyes flashed dangerously. 'And you burnt the toast this morning.'

'Oh, really now—'

'*And* you let Dad go off to the jungle all by himself.'

A heavy silence descended over the kitchen.

'Now, now, Ottillee, I'm going to forget you made a hurtful comment like that,' Mum finally said, her gaze sweeping coolly over me. 'You know very well that Ross always made his own decisions when it came to his work.'

'Sorry, Mum.' I bit my lip, knowing I'd gone too far this time. 'I didn't mean it. That was a horrible thing for me to say.'

'Yes, it was, Ottillee. And just so you know, I've been very proud of your behaviour since we got to Dragondah. Despite this little, erm, morning meltdown.'

'Well, then, can I please go with Finn?'

'No!'

'Why the heck *not?*' And now I was clenching everything on my body it was possible to clench.

'Because you're doing a very good impression of a constipated rabbit right now, that's why the heck not!'

A constipated *rabbit?*

An expectant silence fell over the kitchen as I glanced down at myself. Or rather down at my pink bunny onesie with the fluffy white feet.

And while I unclenched my jaw, my fists and my bottom cheeks, Mum and Finn were doing their best not to smirk. Pretty much like Finn had been doing on and off all morning, to tell you the truth. And then we all burst out laughing.

'So, I'll go and change out of my pyjamas now then, shall I?' I said, backing towards the door with one last toss of my fluffy white ears.

'Yes, Ottillee, and please remember there's more rain forecast, so put on your waterproofs and your wellies like your very sensible friend here.' Mum smiled over at Finn as she picked up her shopping bag. 'Now, young man, before I pop out to Chuggypig for supplies, I want to thank you for casting a spell over my daughter.'

'A spell, Mrs Bottomly?'

'Yes, because thanks to you, she's no longer dying of boredom. And except for the last few minutes, she's no longer driving me up the wall either.'

And as Mum exited the kitchen, I couldn't resist pulling a face behind her back.

———◦◦◇◦◦———

19

'Oh, I Love Rats Me.'

'CAN YOU BELIEVE Lucifer Branson's cheek?' I said to Finn as we made our way down the garden. It was raining again, but I had my hood up so hardly even noticed. 'Pinching your castle from right under your nose like that. Honestly, you just wait — he'll be trying to recruit you for his children's home next!'

Finn shrugged as though he could hardly care less, and I tried again.

'Yeah, it's a good job I never told Mum about you being the *real* owner of Dragondah Castle, hey? She'd have been sure to blab about it to her new *best* friend, and then where the heck would we be, right?'

Another careless shrug.

'I mean, to tell you the truth, I haven't even told Mum about Arlock yet either. I feel really guilty about it because I know I *should* tell her, but then she'd want to meet him, and I'm not sure she'd quite get him—'

'Huh! And your mum wouldn't be the only one, Ottillee!' Finn aimed a vicious kick at a fallen apple, scaring off the speckled crow sheltering from the rain in one of the trees. 'Anyway, I'm sick of talking about Arlock. I'm sick of even thinking about him.'

'Well, I'm sick of thinking about Lucifer Branson,' I retorted as I struggled with the gate into the woods. 'I just wish he'd go back to wherever he came from.'

'Huh! Doesn't sound like that's going to happen any time soon, Ottillee. Not with all his amazing plans for the castle—'

'Yeah, well, he's just going to have to rethink his amazing plans for the castle, isn't he? That place is rightfully yours, Finn, and now we just need to *prove* it. The quicker we find The Dragondah Chronicles, the better—'

'Oh, Ottillee, I wouldn't have a clue where to start looking for that old rubbish.' Finn gave the gate such a hefty push that it opened with ease. 'And what's the point, anyway?'

'You're not serious, Finn?' I grabbed his arm. 'You're not giving up already, are you?'

'But what choice do we have? Arlock's not found The Chronicles in ten years, and now there's this millionaire *phipan — philap—*'

'Philanderer?'

Finn didn't even thank me. 'Yeah, how can we compete

with someone like him? The council certainly seems to think Lucifer Branson's doing us all a favour anyway.'

'A favour?'

'Yeah, he's finally putting the castle to good use, isn't he?'

'Yeah, but it's *you* who should be putting the castle to good use, not him. And, as soon as we've found The Dragondah Chronicles and King Locryn's missing fortune, that's exactly what you're going to be doing.' I ignored Finn's disbelieving snort. 'And you'll certainly do a much better job of it than that horrible person.'

I set off into the woods, only for Finn to grab my arm and hold *me* back this time.

'Tell me why you dislike this man so much, Ottillee. As far as I can tell, your mum's right about him — he *is* a hero, giving orphans a better life, saving his dad from a fire, *and* losing his eye in the process.' Finn dragged me beneath a particularly leafy tree to get us out of the rain. 'And anyway, you only spoke to him for a few minutes, didn't you? Did he do anything so terrible in front of you?'

'Apart from drinking out of Dad's mug, you mean?'

Finn nodded, and I tried to think why I'd taken against Lucifer Branson. So quickly. And so violently.

'Well, he was far too friendly, of course.'

Finn's eye roll told me exactly what he thought about that.

'And he was far too nosy as well. Oh yeah, and he was

really pushy, offering to help Mum with anything she needed.' Reluctantly, I met Finn's gaze. Even *I* realised how stupid I was starting to sound. 'Okay, well, when I think about it, I suppose Lucifer Branson isn't *that* bad.'

'Exactly.' He glanced at me from under his brows. 'If you ask me, Ottillee, you wouldn't like *any* man who offered to help your mum.'

'That's not true!'

'Isn't it?' Finn didn't look convinced. 'Anyway, in my opinion, Arlock's the shifty one round here.'

'Pfft! Now *you're* the one who's being unfair.'

'Well, you've got to admit Arlock's not quite right, is he? Living in a cave. Wearing all that old-fashioned clobber. And he talks nonsense most of the time.'

Mmmm, Finn had certainly been giving Arlock a whole lot of thought while he'd been walking in the rain and gazing up at the stars.

'Yeah, Arlock *is* a bit different, Finn, but what's wrong with that? And anyway, hasn't he just spent the last ten years of his life trying to help *your* family? You shouldn't be giving him a hard time, you know. You should be grateful to him.'

'Oh, grateful, is it? Grateful to someone who ambushes me in a cave? Who kidnaps Vixen and Shadow? Who talks to me in riddles?' Finn was looking anything *but* grateful. 'Honestly, there's something not right about that man.

And I can't get it out of my head that I know him—'

'Well, he did hint that he'd met you before, remember?'

But he shook his head. 'No, that's not it. Arlock *reminds* me of someone I know, that's all.'

I suppressed a heavy sigh and decided to change the subject. I mean, Finn and I were never going to agree over Arlock and Lucifer Branson, were we?

'Hey, I've an idea,' I said as brightly as I could manage. 'Why don't we take a walk over to Dragondah Castle this morning? It does belong to you, remember.'

'Huh!' Finn snorted. 'Tell that to the workers who were trampling all over the place on Sunday! Spotted their high-vis jackets soon as I got home, I did. Lucifer Branson probably sent them, now I come to think about it.'

'What a cheek! What the heck were they doing?'

'Don't know and don't particularly care.' He shrugged. 'Although Nanna Nessa nearly fell into her vegetable patch when I told her what was going on.'

'I'm not surprised! Those people are messing with your family home, Finn!' I was all fired up again now, even if he wasn't. 'Now come on, *please* don't give up on finding The Dragondah Chronicles. And please tell me the only way anyone's getting their hands on that castle is over your dead body!'

Finn looked alarmed, as well as defeated now.

'Oh, Ottillee, I wish it was *you* who was related to King

Locryn instead of me,' he grumbled as he tightened his hood against the worsening weather. 'You'd be so much better at all this royal stuff than I am.'

'Oh, don't be silly,' I replied briskly while secretly thinking Finn had a point. I'd relish being a member of the Penhaligon royal family and would happily put Lucifer Branson in his place. No matter how many orphans or fathers he'd saved. 'Now come on, let's get going.'

I set off into the woods, grateful Mum had made me wear my mac and wellies. After all the rain we'd had these past few days, the path was little more than a quagmire. Yet it was still Finn who was giving me the hardest time.

'Honestly, Ottillee,' I could hear him complaining as he squelched along behind me, 'there's absolutely no point in us traipsing all the way out to the castle in this rain. It's a long walk, a good mile at least. And anyway, I've been over there loads of times already, and there's absolutely nothing to see. Well, nothing but the world's biggest rats, of course—'

'Oh, I *love* rats me,' I trilled as I stepped over a fallen log. 'Back in Bumstead, we once had this rescue rat called Rambo. Dad said he was better for me than a dog because he wouldn't mind being left alone all day. To tell you the truth, Rambo seemed to prefer it when I was at school. Wasn't all that keen on being cuddled, you see.'

This forced Finn to take another approach. 'Yeah, well,

I don't even think we can get to the castle right now. The water was well on its way in earlier.'

'Nice try, Finn, but it's not high tide until two o'clock.' I tossed him a knowing grin over my shoulder. 'Well, according to the tide timetable I found in our library anyway!'

'Even so, there's definitely some really, *really* bad weather on the way.'

This was Finn's last shot at changing my mind, but my only reply was to quicken my pace. At last, he realised he was beaten, and soon the two of us were on the headland staring out across the bay at the towering block of grey stone that was Dragondah Castle. It still looked like it needed rescuing to me.

———◦◦◇◇◦◦———

'Not The Dragon Again?'

'KEEP UP, FINN — not far to go!'

I was trudging across the beach towards the castle. While the mile of rippling sand was mostly behind me now, Finn was still struggling to catch up. Although little wonder. The raindrops were coming down like bullets, and his thin blue anorak was sticking to him like cling film. I mean, maybe it *hadn't* been fair to drag him all the way out here on such a soaking wet day, I couldn't help think as I sidestepped a stranded jellyfish. After all, not everyone was lucky enough to have a brand new mac with a fleece lining, drawstring hood and water-repellent finish, were they?

And then, just like that, I forgot all about the sudden downpour and Finn's useless anorak, not to mention my own second thoughts. I even forgot to close my mouth. Dragondah Castle was now looming high above me, and it was even more impressive close-up than it had been from Dragondah Peek. This was no fairy tale palace built for Penhaligon princesses, I realised. This was a secure fortress built to keep out Penhaligon enemies. The walls rising up from the rocky island base were twice as thick as I was tall. The narrow windows were clearly designed to stop arrows getting in rather than let people see out. And even the birds were hostile out here. A crow was squawking furiously at me from the battlements. The seagulls wheeling about the tower were trying to see which one of them could screech at me the loudest.

But their scare tactics didn't put me off, and I did my best to scramble up the side of the rock, only thankful the rainstorm had finally subsided. But the wet ground was still too slippery, and both my attempts resulted in failure.

'Wellies aren't great for rock climbing, are they, Ottillee?' commented Finn as he helped me to my feet.

'Oh, you're here at last, are you?' I did my best not to giggle at Finn's unintentional owl impression. He'd tied his hood so tightly about his face that only his eyes were visible. 'Anyone would think you didn't *want* to show me your long-lost family home.'

'Huh!' Finn loosened his hood impatiently. 'I'm still not convinced this *is* my long-lost family home.'

'Oh, yeah?' I smiled at him. 'Have you forgotten that carving of your — I mean King Locryn's face on the wall?'

'Oh, yeah, I *had* forgotten about that, as it happens.' Finn suddenly set off. 'So now that you've dragged me out here, there's something I want to see close-up.'

Seconds later, the two of us were huddled together at the foot of the castle's eastern wall trying to make out King Locryn's face in the stone. But no matter how much Finn and I stared and squinted, the carving visible from Dragondah Peek was impossible to detect from this distance. Yes, there were hollows and indentations in the stone, but that's all they were. There was nothing that looked like the eyes, nose, mouth and chin of Cornwall's greatest-ever king. *Or* the boy standing next to me.

'We're standing too close, that's all,' I said briskly, pulling a face at the crow still glaring down at us from the battlements. 'And anyway, it certainly explains why Arlock dragged us all the way up to Dragondah Peek, doesn't it? The man clearly knows what he's talking about.'

My companion snorted rudely, and I could have kicked myself for mentioning Arlock again. So, keen to change the subject, I asked Finn to lead the way into the castle. Strangely, his only response was to glance at the sky, drag off his wet anorak and tie it carefully around his waist. But it was when he started cleaning his fingernails that I knew something was up. It didn't take a genius to work out what.

'You've never actually *been* inside this castle before, have you?' I asked him tightly.

'Erm, nope.' Finn's expression was sheepish when he finally met my gaze. 'To tell you the truth, Nanna Nessa always said the, erm, you-know-what would get me—'

'Oh, no, you've got to be kidding!' I cried. 'Not the shapeshifting dragon again?'

'Yeah, well, how was *I* to know the dragon didn't actually exist, Ottillee?' Finn was looking most put out. 'I was only a kid, and I wasn't going to take any chances, was I?'

I shook my head tiredly, frustrated not with Finn, but with Nanna Nessa herself. Honestly, what the heck was wrong with her? Scaring a boy half to death with her fictitious monsters. Stopping him from having the usual childhood adventures and, even more importantly, stopping him from exploring his *own* family's home. I mean, thank heavens the old lady had realised her mistake just in time and asked *me* to step in.

I grabbed Finn by the hand and led him round the castle walls. Dragondah Island extended much further back than I'd expected, the rock the castle loomed over linked to a flatter piece of grassland by a series of rock pools. It was quite a relief when I spotted the stone steps winding their way up towards the castle gatehouse.

The big black sign saying 'PRIVATE PROPERTY — KEEP OUT!' was much less welcome though. I gazed at it for a long moment, realising it had been put up by order of Lucifer Branson, and seriously considering pushing it over.

'Okay, okay, I know he's turning it into a children's home!' I cried when a horrified Finn clearly read my thoughts and pulled me away. 'It's just not *his* private property though, is it?'

I hurried up the steps after Finn, doing my best to ignore all his dark mutterings. I didn't know what he was darkly muttering about, and I didn't particularly care. The squawking seagulls were also making their annoyance known, every one of them getting on my last nerve. I could only hope matters improved soon.

And what do you know? Finn *did* perk up a bit as we made our way through the castle entrance and into the courtyard. Maybe he was intrigued by the stone dragon peering down at us from the gatehouse? Maybe he was wondering how deep that waterhole was at the edge of the cobbles? Maybe he was imagining Shadow soaring about the circular tower in the dead of night? Or maybe he was wondering why a life-size statue of a ferocious dog was guarding that building at the far end?

Evidence of the recent storm was everywhere, of course, rain still trickling down the ancient stone walls and creating

puddles between the cobblestones. I almost jumped out of my skin when a rat raced past us. Twice the size of my Rambo, it had what looked like a fishtail in its jaws.

'Told you there'd be rats over here, didn't I?' said Finn, promptly relapsing into his bad mood again. 'So what's the plan now then?'

'I'm not sure yet,' I muttered, frowning at yet more of Lucifer Branson's signs. A few said 'DANGER', a few said 'CAUTION — HARD HAT AREA!' but most said, 'PRIVATE PROPERTY — KEEP OUT!'

'You try and make us,' I muttered mutinously as my eyes narrowed on a heavy wooden door at the far end of the courtyard. 'Let's go and explore that big building over there — I'll bet you any money that's where the Penhaligons used to live in the olden days.'

Finn released his heaviest sigh yet, and I desperately tried to think of something to keep him interested.

'You never know, we might get lucky and find The Dragondah Chronicles in there.'

'Oh, yeah, sure,' he mocked. 'Don't you think Arlock would have been all over this place already?'

'Probably, but where's the harm in a bit of a snoop about ourselves?' I pointed towards the statue. 'For all we know, they could be buried beneath that dog over there.'

'That's not a dog, you skogyn, that's a *wolf!*' More scoffing. 'Anyway, it's more likely that rat's just eaten them.'

'Oh, don't be such a sarcy pants, you—'

'Or Nan's got them tucked away in her biscuit tin back home.'

'Honestly, I really—'

'They could even be in your bedroom at Dragondah Hall!'

I sighed. Finn's smart-alecky attitude was *really* getting on my last nerve now.

'Well, wherever they are, Finn *Penhaligon,* they'll turn up eventually, just you mark my words.'

Bolstered by my little dig (I knew the 'Penhaligon' would annoy him), I made my way across the cobbles towards what must be some sort of great hall. Thankfully, its door opened easily enough, and seconds later, Finn and I were wandering about a vast space with uneven flagstones on the floor and timber beams supporting the roof. The iron chandeliers and walk-in fireplace confirmed this was where the Cornish royal family had once lived, the spiral stairway leading up to their sleeping quarters, I assumed.

'Just imagine, Finn,' I said, my voice echoing around the high stone walls, my nose twitching at the unfamiliar musty smell. 'The great King Locryn used to warm himself by this very fire. Probably after righting all Dragondah's wrongs and fighting its dark forces. Oh yes, and after writing something very deep and meaningful in the family archives.'

'Oh, you're talking about your precious Dragondah Chronicles now, are you? I can't see any hiding places for them though, can you?' Finn was wandering about aimlessly, kicking walls to see how strong they were, and sticking his tongue out at the dragon gargoyles glowering down at us from all four corners. Not even the carving above the fireplace seemed to impress him. 'Yeah, you'd have thought Cornwall's greatest ever king would have left more than this stupid plaque behind, wouldn't you?'

'Oh, honestly, Finn, that's your family crest, that is!'

'My family *crest?*'

'Yeah, all royal families have family crests.' I walked over and peered up at his. 'Yeah, yours has got a dragon on it, while the British royal family — well, theirs has got a lion on it. And a horse. Or it might be a deer. Or even a unicorn, I can't remem—'

'Yeah, yeah.' Finn couldn't have sounded less interested. 'It's just I was expecting — well, more furniture, I suppose. Maybe even some family paintings. A throne or two, at the very least.'

'Oh, Finn, all that stuff would have been moved centuries ago. Or maybe even stolen, hey?' My gaze landed on the steps in the corner. 'Although maybe we'll have more luck up there, what do you think?'

A begrudging nod, and seconds later, I was leading Finn past more 'DANGER' and 'KEEP OUT' signs up the spiral stairway of the tower. But the rooms on the two floors we passed yielded little more than empty fireplaces, cooing doves and scurrying mice. Although there was an ancient toilet in one of them, confirming Arlock's assertion that the Penhaligons had done what they could to maintain the castle. And then suddenly, the steady thump-thump-thump of some kind of motor filled the air.

'What's that?' I asked suspiciously, some sixth sense telling me this wasn't good news. The noise was getting louder by the second, but Finn simply shrugged it away.

'Oh, that sounds like a helicopter, that does. Probably just some sightseeing emmets.'

'Sightseeing *hermits?*'

'No, emmets, Ottillee, *emmets.* You know, people who don't come from round here.'

'But I thought they — sorry, *we* were called blow-ins?'

'No, Ottillee, blow-ins actually *live* in Cornwall like you and your mum. Emmets are only here on holiday. You know, usually at one of the beach resorts further down the coast.'

'Oh, right, gotcha.' Cripes, there was so much new stuff to learn in Cornwall. And then something occurred to me. 'Would herm — I mean *emmets* be sightseeing on a rainy day like this though?'

'Course they would, Ottillee. Because if it was sunny, they'd be tanning themselves on the sands, wouldn't they?' The thump-thump-thump sound had suddenly stopped, and Finn's attention was now elsewhere. 'What do we have here?'

We'd reached the top floor of the tower. A wooden door with large dragon-shaped hinges was blocking our way, and I couldn't help gasp with a sudden realisation. Because I'd seen that door before, hadn't I? At Dragondah Peek when the light had gone all strange. When the castle had appeared so much closer than it actually was.

Finn and I exchanged looks. He was clearly as intrigued as I was. I tried the door first, but it wouldn't budge. Finn stepped forwards, placed his shoulder against it and pushed as hard as he could. The door fell open, as did our mouths.

The bedchamber on the other side of it was as dusty and musty as expected, but it was also furnished which was a total surprise. Even more astonishing, the four-poster bed in the middle of the room was still made up, a couple of pillows at its head, and a purple bedspread falling in folds to the floor.

Finn and I advanced across the flagstones, our eyes taking in the antique chests, the iron candelabras, the faded tapestries and the large fireplace which was now empty of everything but cobwebs. Endless views were on offer through the grimy, salt-spattered windows. Dragondah's advancing tide could be seen on one side, while on the other side were its woodlands, rolling fields and sheer cliffs. Yet it was still the four-poster bed that drew our gaze. Not because it was centre stage, but because it was a work of art complete with hand-carved posts and a multi-peaked canopy.

'Oh, my gosh, Finn, can you believe you were *born* in this bed?'

'I was?'

'Yeah, don't you remember? Arlock said you were born in the king's bedchamber.' I plumped up one of the pillows, its white cotton cover threadbare and yellowing with age but still edged with pretty lace. 'I mean, he's the one who's probably been keeping an eye on everything in here. I *told* you that you should be grateful to him, didn't I?'

'Crikey.' Finn stepped forward for a closer look, and I could only imagine the thoughts that were going through his head as his fingers smoothed the velvet bedspread.

'Yeah, it's almost too much to take in, isn't it?' I reached out to stroke one of the intricate shapes etched into the nearest bedpost. 'And what are these designs? They're so pretty, aren't they?'

Finn peered closer. 'They look like love knots to me.'

'*Love* knots?'

He couldn't help chuckle at my embarrassed expression.

'Oh, get away with you, Ottillee! Love knots are ancient Cornish symbols, that's all — you know, to signify the everlasting love between two people. They're very romantic, they are.'

Finn didn't seem at all embarrassed to be talking about such things, but I could feel myself blushing. I knew it was childish, but lovey-dovey stuff always got me flustered when I was talking to boys. And then suddenly, the lovey-dovey stuff didn't matter anymore. I could hear voices. And even worse than that, I could also hear footsteps.

———◦◦◊◦◦———

21

'Bit Of A Whinge Bag Too.'

'SOMEONE'S COMING!' Finn hissed. 'What are we going to do, Ottillee? We really shouldn't be here.'

'We have every right to be here!' I hissed back, trying to ignore the 'DANGER' and 'KEEP OUT' signs flashing before my eyes. King Locryn's bedchamber was getting darker by the minute, another downpour clearly on its way. 'You own this castle, Finn Penhaligon, you *own* it!'

Yet despite my bold claims, I must admit to growing feelings of panic. The voices were getting louder, and there was no doubt the new arrivals were aiming straight for this room. Finn and I were trapped.

'Honestly, Dagger, you could have used a sick bag,' we could hear a man complaining now. 'Lizard-skin loafers don't come cheap, you know. Handmade especially for me, these were.'

'Sorry, Mr Lucifer, sir,' another male voice rang out. 'Who knew helicopters could make such sudden moves?

Dropped like a stone, it did.'

'Oh, pooh on a stick!' I cursed in shocked dismay. 'It wasn't *emmets* in that helicopter, Finn. It was Lucifer Branson and one of his men.'

'Phew!' Finn pretended to wipe the sweat off his brow. 'What a relief, Ottillee! I thought we were in big trouble for a moment.'

'Humph! We still might be!'

'Giss on!' Finn scoffed. 'A nice man like Lucifer Branson isn't going to be bothered by the likes of us. Let's just say our hellos and tell him we got lost.'

But something, I don't know what, was telling me this wasn't a good idea. 'No,' I whispered, my panicked eyes darting all about the room. There was only one option. 'Let's hide under the bed until they leave.'

'What the heck do you think you're *doing,* Ottillee?'

'Trust me, will you?' I scuttled beneath the four-poster, leaving Finn with little choice but to join me in the dusty darkness.

'Honestly, Ottillee, I know you don't like the man, but this is ridiculous!'

'Hey, lower your voice, will you?'

'Ach-ooo!'

'And breathe through your mouth, you skogyn!' I pulled the bedspread down so that Finn and I only had a spider's eye view of the room. 'I mean, who knows what Lucifer

Branson will do if he finds us snooping about the place? And no one else knows we've even *come* here, remember?'

Ten seconds later, the door to the room was pushed wide open, and two sets of feet appeared. One set (wearing shiny brown loafers with no socks) clearly belonged to Lucifer Branson. The other set (wearing navy sandals with white socks) clearly belonged to his employee, Dagger.

'I could have sworn we shut that door the last time we were here,' Lucifer Branson said as he walked over to the window. His voice was as deep as I remembered from our first meeting, just nowhere near as warm and friendly. 'And I told those workmen not to come anywhere *near* this bedchamber.'

'Oh, we probably just forgot to shut it ourselves, sir,' grovelled Dagger. 'Got a sudden vermin sighting, if you recall?'

'Don't remind me,' Lucifer Branson snapped. 'I can't believe you've not trapped that little pest yet. If we aren't careful, the council will be getting wind of it. We can only hold them off for so long, you know.'

Finn and I exchanged glances. It wasn't looking good for that poor rat we'd spotted earlier.

'Oh, I've got it all in hand, sir, believe me. You just concentrate on getting *yourself* set up.' Dagger strolled over to straighten the bedspread above our heads. 'If I remember rightly, you weren't sure whether this was going to be your room or you wanted to be nearer the Great Hall, remember?'

Lucifer Branson's loafers swivelled round to join Dagger's sandals by the bed. 'Oh, this room has definitely got my name on it, Dagger. Nice and private, and I can keep an eye on the whole coastline from here. No one will be able to make a move without me seeing them. And anyway, if it was good enough for Locryn the Loathsome—'

'Oh, that's a good one, sir!'

'Yes, if it was good enough for that Penhaligon pretender, then it's certainly good enough for me.'

My eyes widened at the contempt in Lucifer Branson's voice when he spoke about Finn's ancestor. Locryn the *Loathsome,* hey? The Penhaligon *pretender?* So much for 'giving the castle's history all the respect it deserved', as he'd promised in *The Cornish Clarion.* I desperately wanted to see how Finn was responding to all this, but I was too scared to turn my head. In fact, I was too scared to breathe in case the dust got up my nose.

'And will you be sleeping in this bed, sir?' I heard Dagger ask now. 'Because I've no idea how we're going to move it otherwise. It must weigh a ton.'

'Good heavens, Dagger, what on earth are you thinking? This isn't a bed. This is firewood.'

'Another good one, sir!' Dagger chuckled. 'You're going to use your new chainsaw on it, are you?'

'Got it on one, Dagger. As soon as we've got electricity over here, it'll give me great pleasure to turn this decaying Penhaligon symbol to dust.' Lucifer Branson banged the bed so hard that the massive structure shuddered above our heads. 'Love knots and all.'

'Good job, sir!' Dagger's voice was suddenly rather sly. 'Pity you can't do the same to that little—'

'Now, now, Dagger, I keep telling you. I need to make sure first. Anyway, I've asked about, and he hasn't a clue what's going on. Hardly seems to know what day it is, to tell you the truth! So, let's just play it carefully and stick to our plan.'

'Yes, but what a relief when it's all over, hey?'

'When we can get back to doing what we're good at, you mean?'

'Exactly.'

Totally confused now, I sneaked a look at Finn. His only reaction was a tightening of his mouth.

'Do you really think we can do it this time, Dagger?' I heard Lucifer Branson ask, a surprising hint of uncertainty in his tone. 'Do you really think we can smooth out our last few little problems?'

'Well, I've done *my* bit, sir. The council's playing ball, the building materials are on order, and the trap is set—'

'In more ways than one, hey?'

'Exactly.' Dagger's voice turned sly again. 'But tell me,

how did you get on at Dragondah Hall?'

'Oh, it's too early to say, but at least I got through the front door this time. The beautiful Grace Bottomly was a welcome change from that sour-faced caretaker, let me tell you. She even invited me in for a chat. Although with a daughter like hers, little wonder she was happy to see a friendly face!'

'A bit of a madam, was she?'

'No, a bit of a nightmare more like! Dressed in black and throwing me evils every time I took so much as a sip of coffee.'

'Humph! Needs a good walloping that one does! Any idea why she inherited the house in the first place?'

'Not a clue, and neither does anyone else seem to know either. Anyway, it's no problem, Dagger. I'll just work a bit more magic on the grieving widow, and I'll have the run of the place in no time. Thankfully, there are no *other* family members around to get in my way.'

Now I really was aghast. I *knew* Lucifer Branson wasn't to be trusted. Not only was he up to something dodgy with the castle, but he was up to something dodgy with my mother too! I'd have dragged myself out from under the bed had Finn not grabbed hold of my sleeve and mouthed, 'No!' I pushed him off but, to his obvious relief, stayed where I was. Then it didn't seem to matter much anyway.

'Something's going on in here,' I suddenly heard Dagger

say, his voice a furtive whisper. 'I can hear noises under the bed. Do you think we've got mice?'

'Cockroaches, more like!' Lucifer Branson's voice held a trace of relish. He laughed when Dagger launched himself onto the bed, the mattress squeaking in protest above our heads.

'Sorry, sir, but I *hate* cockroaches, I do! Nasty, scuttling little things they are.'

'Good heavens! And to think I put a man like you in charge of pest control!'

A scornful Lucifer Branson stepped away, only to return seconds later. 'Watch and learn, Dagger,' he said before kneeling down and lifting up the bedspread right in front of our noses. 'This is the way to deal with uninvited guests.'

Finn and I exchanged terrified glances at the sight of the heavy candelabra in Lucifer Branson's hairy hand. We knew we were cornered. We knew we were done for. And then, just as we were bracing ourselves for discovery at best and a beating at worst, the sound of the helicopter's whirring blades filled the air. Lucifer Branson hesitated for what seemed like an eternity before straightening up with an angry curse.

'Too late, Dagger. Must be another storm on the way.' He banged threateningly on the bedpost. 'You live to fight another day, cockroaches! But be warned, your days are numbered. Dragondah Castle's got itself a new king now!'

Finn and I could only stare at each other wordlessly as the two sets of footsteps echoed away from us down the tower. Both of us were trying to make sense of what we'd just heard. Not that we could, of course, our only option to shimmy out from beneath the bed as soon as we deemed it safe.

'You were right all along, Ottillee,' Finn said as he straightened up and brushed the dust from his clothes. His face was even whiter than usual, although whether from shock or anger, I didn't know. 'That man's certainly no hero.'

I didn't reply at first. I didn't even say, 'I told you so'. I was still reeling from everything I'd just heard. Lucifer Branson's disdain for his employee. His contempt for the Cornish royal family. His frustration the poor rat was still alive. His glee at being able to spy on everyone from the top of the tower. Not to mention his arrogant plan to — well, *marry* my mother when she was still grieving for my dad.

'Do you know what *I* think?' I said as I pulled a cobweb out of Finn's hair.

'What?' He pulled an even longer one out of mine.

'That Lucifer Branson's nothing but a big old bully. I know the type, let me tell you. He just wants to lord it over everyone at the school—'

'The school?'

'Sorry, I mean the *castle*.'

'Yeah, he does seem to know a lot about this place, doesn't he? You know, considering he doesn't come from round here. He certainly fancies himself as the new King Locryn anyway.'

'Although did you hear what he called the king? Loathsome, he called him. And a pretender, whatever the heck *that* is.'

'Yeah, it's as if he didn't think the king *deserved* his title.' Finn's mouth twisted wryly. 'Can you imagine what Lucifer Branson would do if someone like me claimed to be the king's heir and the *real* owner of this castle?'

'Laugh in your face probably.'

'Yeah, what a bit of luck you didn't tell your mum about me, hey? She'd have been sure to let on to him.'

'Yeah, but only because she's so trusting, Finn.' I found myself sticking up for Mum. 'And she gets nervous with new people, you know. Tells them all sorts of inappropriate things over mugs of coffee.'

'Mmmm, Lucifer Branson does seem quite keen on her, I noticed.' Finn looked at me from under his lashes. 'Not you so much though.'

'Huh! Who cares about that? And as for my mum, he's got zero chance with her. She's still head over heels in love with my dad and always will be. No, it's Lucifer Branson's orphans, I'm worried about. Can you image what he's going to put the poor things through?'

'Yeah, he'll probably make them call him *King* Lucifer.'

'And clean his lizard-skin shoes every morning.'

'And polish his swanky gold watch.'

'And clip his toenails.'

'And peel his grapes.'

'And brush his big teeth with a scrubbing brush!'

'And wipe his nose! And his—'

'EEEEEE-YEW, enough!' I wrinkled my own nose in disgust. 'I mean, we've just got to stop him opening that children's home, haven't we?'

'Yeah, and not just for us, but for the poor kids as well. Ooops! Watch out!'

This as Finn dragged me to the floor. The helicopter was now hovering outside the window, almost as though its occupants were double-checking the bedchamber was still empty. But thankfully, it flew off after a few seconds, the steady thump of its rotary blades fading into the distance.

'Phew, that was a close one!' Finn hoisted me to my feet. 'They nearly spotted us there!'

'Yeah, best we keep well out of Lucifer Branson's way for now, right? The next time we see him we want to be waving the deeds to Dragondah Castle in his face, okay?'

'That suits me fine, Ottillee. And don't you worry, I've got the measure of that one now.' Finn's expression turned grim. 'Lucifer Branson might have fooled the local council and the local newspaper—'

'And even the local mums—'

'Exactly. But he's not fooled Finn Penhaligon, has he?'

'Oh, Finn *Penhaligon* now, is it?' I managed a smile. 'Well, at least two good things have come out of today.'

'Oh, yeah? Like what?'

'Well, number one, you've finally accepted who you are.'

'Mmmm, and number two?'

'You've also discovered your fighting spirit!'

A long silence before Finn released a heartfelt sigh.

'You're right, Ottillee. I'm sorry I've been such a—'

'Namby-pamby fraidy-cat?'

'Ouch, bit harsh, isn't it?'

'Grumpy old git then?'

'Yeah, sorry.'

'Bit of a whinge bag too?'

'I suppose.'

'And what about a crankypants?'

'Mmmm, I'll give you that one as well.'

'And don't forget grumpy old git.'

'You said that one already, Ottillee. And yes, I get it. I have been all those things. But that was before I discovered Lucifer Branson was a big bully who really doesn't *deserve* Dragondah Castle.' His mouth tightened. 'And the only way he's getting his mitts on it now *is* over my dead body.'

'That's the attitude, Finn! Give me five!' I realised too late that he didn't know what I was talking about, but who cared? I picked myself off the floor and beamed at him. 'Now, let's meet again tomorrow, and come up with a plan to beat that horrid man, okay? Say, my kitchen, ten o'clock?'

'Okay, sure.' Finn looked at me under his lashes. 'You really think we can beat him, Ottillee?'

'Course we can.' I gave him a reassuring pat on the shoulder. 'All we've got to do is find The Dragondah Chronicles, haven't we?'

I wasn't sure, but I think I saw Finn wince.

———◦◦◊◦◦———

22

Dad's Secret Report

DATE: Monday, 13 August, 2018   TIME: 9 pm

PLACE: Bedroom, of course   SUBJECT: An update

Dear Dad,

A quick one this time, just to fill you in on all the latest developments...

1) My instincts were right, as usual!! Mum's friend is a shifty stinker. He might be turning the castle into a children's home, but only so he can live like a king and boss everyone about. I mean, if he bullies his orphans like he bullies his staff, a mass breakout is guaranteed!! He's also planning to chainsaw King Locryn's beautiful bed (the bed where Finn was born!!), and he prefers his animals when they're dead — he's not just a cockroach clubber and a rat trapper, but he's also happy to wear fancy shoes made from murdered lizards that are very probably on the endangered species list. Let's hope he never gets his hands on the local seals, hey?

2) Lucifer Branson fancies his chances with Mum too. He even called her 'beautiful', if you can believe his cheek?! But don't worry, because I've checked with her, and she doesn't share his feelings in any way whatsoever. (Certainly not in a girlfriend/boyfriend/love-knot kind of way.) And I have to admit that the most she's done is make him hot beverages and tell him every single thing about our lives. So you'll understand why I'm STILL being careful what I say to her right now. Certainly nothing about Finn being the heir to the long-lost Cornish throne and the real owner of Dragondah Castle. Because something tells me Lucifer Branson's not the kind of man to give up the castle without a fight.

3) The good news is I'm not having to deal with all this by myself anymore. And that's because FINN'S BACK IN DRAGONDAH!!!!! Hip, hip, hooray!! The even better news is that he's finally accepted he's a Penhaligon. And the even better news is that he's a million per cent ready to fight for his castle!!! Yes, I'm sure it won't be long before the two of us have come up with an ace plan to find The Dragondah Chronicles and get our hands on those castle deeds. Then we can tell Mum's shifty stinker to get lost/beat it/go jump in the lake/take a long walk off a short pier!!!

Lots of love, as always.
And a big sloppy 'mwah' from your mergh*!!!
Ottillee xoxoxo

* Mergh means 'daughter' in Cornish, just in case you can't guess. I'm also now learning the months of the year (right tongue-twisters!) and will soon be moving on to 'Animals & Birds'. Yes, it's amazing what you can get done when you don't have a telly or a laptop. (Maybe <u>certain</u> people would get in touch with me if they weren't always looking for rare stamps online or watching junior baking shows.) Honestly, Dad, I'm beginning to suspect Mrs Gupta's the only one in Bumstead who knows how to write a letter?!!

23

'What Are The Dragondah Chronicles?'

WHEN FINN SHOWED up at Dragondah Hall the following morning, I stuck a mug of tea in his right hand and a delicious homemade treat in his left.

'Come on, Finn, it's not going to kill you, you know!'

Honestly, he was inspecting the fairy cake (made during my Tudor wench period) as if it was booby-trapped. He'd even twisted his cap round to the back of his head for extra safety.

'But what are those pink and green things on top, Ottillee?'

'They're sprinkles, of course. Totally harmless they are. Full of vitamins too, most likely.' I rolled my eyes when Finn sniffed the cake again. 'Now, will you *please* get a move on or Mum will have finished her bath.'

'But what's the rush?' Finn kept sipping his tea, his eyes darting about the kitchen as though we had all the time in the world. 'Oh, that's your dad's football mug, is it?'

I nodded, sighing when he went over to peer at the framed photo next to it.

'And who are *these* people?'

'Oh, the dark-haired one with the beard is my dad. He was getting an award from the famous, erm, wildlife documentary maker Sir Michael Rabbit-Burrows–'

'*Rabbit*-Burrows?'

'Yeah, that's what Dad and I used to call him anyway.' I was anxious to move on. 'Anyway, as soon as you've finished your, erm, mouthwatering snack, we're going to go and track Arlock down.'

Finn pulled a face. 'But I thought we were coming up with a plan of our own, Ottillee?'

'Well, yes, we are, but there's still so much we don't know, isn't there?' My hands were on my hips, my patience running thin. 'Arlock's the only one who can give us proper information about The Dragondah Chronicles, isn't he?'

'Like what?'

I brought a list out of my pocket. Not *that* long, I didn't think.

'Well, number one, what *are* The Dragondah Chronicles? Are we looking for some sort of old book like that one Arlock threw away? Or are they, you know, more like a collection of separate documents? Maybe hidden away in an old wooden chest?'

'Like a treasure chest, you mean?'

Finn's eyes flashed, but I managed to suppress my own excitement, determined to keep things professional.

'Yes, and number two, we want to know where Arlock's already looked for these Chronicles. I mean, we don't want to waste our time looking in all the same places, do we?'

'Fair enough.' Finn was now nibbling on the cake as if he was nibbling on a piece of coal. I tried to keep my mind on the task at hand.

'And then there's this children's home at the castle. Did Arlock know about it? And if so, why didn't he tell *us?*'

Finn pulled a face, and this time I snatched the cake out of his hand.

'Honestly, Finn, you do get on my last nerve sometimes. I baked those cakes myself, and they're only five days old. What the heck's wrong—?'

'Oh, there's nothing's wrong with your baking, Ottillee.' Finn snatched the cake back and swallowed it in one gulp. 'It's Arlock I've got the problem with.'

'Why? What's he done *now?*'

'Well, you're wondering why he never told us about the children's home, aren't you? But he never tells us *anything* really, does he? Just drops loads of stupid hints. You know, like he's met me before. Like he knew my parents. Oh yeah, and then there was all that stuff about the "dark forces circling again".'

Finn rolled his eyes. 'Honestly, Ottillee, have you ever heard such twaddle in your whole life?'

'Well, yes I have, if I'm honest with you. Your own nan was saying the same sort of thing about Dragondah not so very long ago. Going on about "the forces of good and evil". And us all being "plunged into darkness" if we weren't careful. And at least Arlock's not mentioned any shapeshifting dragons yet, has he?'

'I suppose not.'

'Yeah, and you've got to admit that everything Arlock's told us has been right so far. I mean, Nanna Nessa's confirmed you're a Penhaligon. And we've seen the bedchamber where you were born with our very own eyes. What more do you—?'

'Yeah, that's all well and good, Ottillee, but I still know Arlock's hiding something. And I just can't get over the effect he's had on my animals. Shadow only comes home to sleep nowadays. Although at least he's got over his cold, which is something I suppose—'

'Yes, exactly.'

'And as for Vixen, well, she hardly leaves Arlock's side—'

'But doesn't that tell you something, Finn?' I cried. His resentment was understandable, but it was also very tiresome. 'Your animals trust Arlock, so why don't you?'

Finn's sullen shrug told me I was fighting a losing battle, so I took a deep calming breath and tried another tack.

'You trust me though, don't you, Finn?'

'Course.'

'Then trust me when I say we can't make any progress until we've spoken to Arlock.' I could hear Mum making her way down the stairs, so I picked up Dad's torch and brandished it in the air. 'And before you start moaning again, we're going to go and find Arlock along the secret tunnel.'

Finn's eyes lit up. '*Now* you're talking, Ottillee!'

And just seconds before Mum joined us in the kitchen and started asking her usual tricky questions, I was leading Finn into the pantry, through the little white door, down the stone steps, and into the tunnel. Finn's eyes followed the beam of the Blaze-100 as I passed it over the tunnel's arched walls.

'Blithering barnacles! What an icebox this place is!' he couldn't help comment with a shiver. 'And it must have taken them forever to dig it out. Say what you like, Ottillee, but those Crows were a clever bunch, weren't they?'

'No, they weren't, Finn. They were a *loathsome* bunch. Rotten to the very depths of their souls.'

Yes, at the thought of what this place had been used for in the past, I couldn't help shiver myself. Somehow I just *knew* the Crows had dragged dead bodies through this tunnel, not just smuggled loot. Finn seemed to sense my unease and grabbed me by the hand.

'Come on, Ottillee, the quicker we find Arlock, the quicker we can get out of here.'

We started running, the echo of our footsteps and the beam of our torch surely announcing our arrival. But when we emerged into the cavern five minutes later, it was to find no one there waiting for us. Arlock's possessions were all neatly tucked away on their ledge.

'Oh, drat! I really thought he'd *be* here.'

Strangely, Finn looked even more disappointed than me. 'Could he be outside on the beach?' he suggested, but I shook my head. It was high tide, and the waves could clearly be heard pounding against the rocks outside.

'Dragondah Peek then?'

I shook my head. 'There's no way Arlock would drag himself up there if he didn't have to. And anyway, why bother when—'

But I never got to finish my sentence. While I'd been talking, I'd been lighting up the cavern's shadowy corners with my torch. Suddenly I'd picked out Shadow. The bat was climbing the walls slowly and steadily as if trying not to draw attention to himself. Vixen was crouched on the ground beneath him, also trying to make herself invisible. Not that Finn noticed anything amiss. Not to begin with anyway.

'I might have known you two reprobates would be hiding in here,' he cried with undisguised joy. 'Come and say hello, the pair of you. I hate to admit it, but I've missed you both!'

'Wait, Finn!' I cautioned as he darted over to them. Because it was obvious to me that neither animal was sharing his delight. Shadow was clinging to the wall now, his body motionless, his face turned away. And although Vixen managed a listless wag of her tail, she didn't bother to get to her feet. A few seconds later, even Finn had got the message.

'Come on, Ottillee, let's get out of here,' he muttered with a wounded look over his shoulder. 'Arlock's nowhere to be seen, and what those two are up to is anyone's guess.'

I nodded, as upset as he was by Shadow and Vixen's furtive behaviour. What *was* it about this cavern? I couldn't help wonder as I hurried back along the tunnel after Finn. It seemed to have a very odd attraction for Dragondah's creatures. Not to mention a very odd effect on them. Just as I'd thought we were finally making progress, things were suddenly starting to spiral out of control.

———◦◦◇◦◦———

'Oh, Honestly, Mum!'

FINN AND I exchanged relieved looks when we emerged into Dragondah Hall's kitchen five minutes later. But our relief was short-lived. A man's legs were sticking out from under the sink at the other end of the room. Mum was hovering about nearby, a wrench in her hand and a smile on her face. She was looking tickled pink by something the man had just said, and alarm bells immediately began ringing in my head. I glanced at Finn to see that he was looking equally apprehensive.

Then as soon as we got a good look at the man's shoes, his *lizard-skin* shoes, our worst fears were confirmed. That was no plumber under our sink. That was Lucifer Branson. He was 'working his magic' on my poor deluded mother again by doing odd jobs about the house.

'Don't worry, Finn,' I whispered. 'He's got no idea you own the castle, remember? All he knows is that you're an orphan—'

'But I'm *not* an orphan, Ottillee. I've got Nanna Nessa looking after me, haven't I?'

'Yeah, sorry, course you have.' This wasn't the time to argue, and I led Finn to a seat at the table. 'Anyway, if he *does* try recruiting you for his children's home, just ignore him. In fact, best you don't say anything at all. He'll probably be leaving soon anyway.'

But I was wrong. When Lucifer Branson heaved himself out from under the sink, not only did my mother wave a couple of teabags in his face, but he nodded gratefully. Mum was quite taken aback to see Finn and me waiting at the table.

'Oh, I was *so* worried the pair of you had gone missing!' she trilled, not looking at all worried as she took the milk out of the fridge. 'Would you like a brew too?'

'Nope,' I snapped just as someone else said, 'Yes, please, Mrs Bottomly.'

Drat! I'd told Finn to keep a low profile! Lucifer Branson's head shot round, and for a moment, he looked like all his Christmases had come at once. And then his one good eye narrowed on Finn, putting me in mind of a hunter sizing up an unsuspecting rabbit. (Or the head of an orphanage sizing up an unsuspecting orphan.) Seconds later, he'd plonked himself down at the table opposite him.

'Ottillee's friend, Finn, I presume?' he asked with a casualness that didn't fool me.

Finn's only reply was a curt nod, but if Lucifer Branson picked up on his lack of respect, he didn't show it. He simply smiled his thanks at Mum as she placed the teacups and a plate of my fairy cakes on the table in front of him. Then before she could return with the teapot, he turned to me.

'What a pity, Ottillee,' he whispered. 'Seems I've got to make do with the best china today. And I did so enjoy drinking out of your father's cheap mug the other morning.'

I couldn't help gasp at such deliberate nastiness, only for Lucifer Branson's grin to flash even wider and whiter. And then, just as quickly, he lost interest in baiting me and returned his attention to his other victim.

'I was hoping our paths would cross sooner rather than later,' he said to Finn, smiling at Mum as she sat down next to him and poured out the teas. 'Because I believe you lost your parents some time back?'

'Yeah, but Finn doesn't need your new children's home,' I interjected sharply, only for Lucifer Branson to carry on like I wasn't even there.

'Because I was thinking my new children's home — sorry, *academy* would be perfect for you.' He threw the suggestion out lightly as though he was offering Finn nothing more than some milk in his tea. 'No doubt you've heard about my plans for the castle, and you're fully entitled to a place over there, aren't you?'

'Entitled?' Finn's wide eyes mirrored my own.

'Yes, you were born round these parts, weren't you?'

'Oh, erm, yes — yes, I was.'

'Then you could get my new venture up and running, so to speak. I'd be honoured to take a fine young lad like you under my wing.'

'But Finn doesn't *want* to be taken under your wing—'

'Don't be so rude, sweetheart.'

I scowled at Mum. 'What I *meant* to say was that he's already under his nanna's wing.'

Lucifer Branson didn't miss a beat, his gaze still on Finn.

'That's all well and good, young man, but does this nanna of yours let you play the latest video games? Or sail dinghies along the coast? Or watch your favourite football team on a 75-inch TV screen with high-definition and surround-sound speakers?'

'Well, not *so* far, she hasn't. Ouch!'

This as Finn received a sneaky kick on the ankle.

'Oh, Ottillee, please let Finn speak for himself,' Mum scolded me again. 'You never know, maybe he'd like to give Lucifer's new academy a try? Maybe his nan would be all for it too? Even you admitted she was getting on a bit now.'

'Oh, honestly, Mum!'

Now I felt like giving *her* a sneaky kick on the ankle. But I never got the chance because Lucifer Branson pounced on Mum's words.

'Yes, lad, before you know it, it won't be your nan looking after you, but *you* looking after your nan.'

I held my breath as I waited for Finn's reply. Surely he wasn't falling for any of this, was he? But I needn't have worried.

'I'd be happy to look after my nan if she got sick.' Finn's voice was steady, and he met Lucifer Branson's gaze full-on. 'It'd be the least I could do, seeing how she's looked after me my whole life.'

Silence descended over the kitchen. Mum was clearly touched by Finn's words, just as Lucifer Branson was irritated by them. He sipped his tea thoughtfully, so thoughtfully I could almost hear the cogs whirring in his brain. And I was right to be suspicious.

'Yes, well, I just didn't want you to miss out on a place, young man, that's all. We've already had quite a bit of interest, I'm delighted to say.' He gave Finn's hand a reassuring pat. 'Anyway, can you please remind me of your last name again? Just so I can instruct my office not to bother you.'

My mouth tightened. What cruel games Lucifer Branson loved to play. As far as *he* was aware, Finn didn't know what his last name was. The big bully was just trying to humiliate him for turning down his dinghies and his video games and his swanky tellies. Thankfully Mum came to the rescue.

'Oh, Lucifer, there can't be too many Finns in this part of Cornwall, can there? I'm sure one name will be more than enough for your office.' She held out the plate of fairy cakes and smiled around the table. 'Now, who's for one of Ottillee's culinary masterpieces?'

'Oh, no!'

'No thanks!'

Lucifer Branson's refusal was loud, but someone else's was even louder. Honestly, the cheek of it! No wonder Finn asked Mum for the nearest toilet and was out through the door before I could stuff one of my culinary masterpieces down his T-shirt! And now it was Lucifer Branson's turn to get to his feet.

'Okay, Gracey, I'm so sorry to abandon you, but it's high time I was getting along too.' *Gracey?* And he was talking as if Mum would struggle to get through the next few hours without him. 'But I'll do my best to get my hands on those special oil paints you're after. Oh yes, and don't forget about tomorrow, okay?'

'How kind you are, Lucifer. And yes, I promise I'll see what I can do to get the — I mean, more *people* to join us.' Mum avoided my eyes as she cleared away the dishes. 'And thanks again for all your help with the blocked sink this morning. What *would* I have done without you?'

But before Lucifer Branson could answer, another voice piped up. A particularly *hoarse* voice. And it was coming through the half-open window.

'You could have asked *me* to help you, Mrs Bottomly. It would have been my pleasure.'

'Oh, my giddy aunt!'

'Who the devil's that?'

'You're *here!*'

'CAW! CAW! CROOOOAK!'

And little wonder the speckled crow was having a hissy fit outside, Mum and Lucifer Branson looking equally mystified in the kitchen. Arlock was now peering at us through the window, his hair a wild tangle about his face, the collar of his coat pulled high about his neck.

I dashed over to lead our unexpected visitor inside and thought fast as I made the rather tricky introduction.

'Erm, this is Arlock, everyone. He's, erm, an old friend of Nanna Nessa's.'

'A pleasure to meet you, Mrs Bottomly.' Arlock smiled tightly as he loosened his coat. 'Sorry for setting off that malevolent old raven up on your roof!'

Oh, so the speckled crow was actually a speckled *raven*, was it? Who knew? Or even cared? Arlock's cold had clearly settled on his chest now, his voice straining painfully when he greeted Mum. Tellingly, he didn't pay any attention to Lucifer Branson, not even responding to his curt nod. And, of course, Mum being Mum, she didn't pick up on the sudden tension in the kitchen.

'Okay, Lucifer, we'll see you tomorrow morning then,' she said cheerfully.

'Yes, right,' came Lucifer Branson's distracted reply as though he'd forgotten she was even there. 'I'll let myself out through the front door if that's okay? My jeep's parked right outside.'

I breathed a sigh of relief as Lucifer Branson finally left us in peace. Mum shared a few polite words with Arlock, although I could tell she was just itching to brush his hair. But as soon as Finn returned to the kitchen a few minutes later, she mumbled something about sorting out her paints and disappeared upstairs.

Finally! Arlock was available for questioning, and I sat down opposite him at the kitchen table.

———◦◦◇◦◦———

'You're A Mind Reader, Arlock.'

'YOU'RE A MIND READER, Arlock, honestly you are! You couldn't have come at a better time.'

'That's an understatement if ever I heard one, young lady,' Arlock wheezed. 'What in God's name was that man doing at Dragondah Hall?'

'Oh, yeah, he's a horror, isn't he? He's after Mum, that's all.' I did my best impression of someone throwing up. 'Although can you believe he's opening that—?'

But Arlock's attention was elsewhere now, his dark eyes narrowing on Finn who'd plonked himself down next to me. 'At least *you* had the good sense to keep out of his way, lad.'

I was about to admit that wasn't *quite* true when the back door swung back on its hinges. Vixen launched herself at Finn, and I was pleased to see him reward her with an affectionate stroke. I was less pleased when he popped my last fairy cake into her mouth, but this wasn't the time to make a fuss.

'Sorry, Ottillee, I forgot I promised Vixen a drink on the way up here.' Arlock managed another tight smile, clearly making an effort to throw off his dour mood. 'Do you think your mother would throw a fit if she found Cornwall's only silver fox in your kitchen?'

'Course not,' I replied, confident my mother would know nothing about it. I placed a bowl of water on the floor for Vixen and the kettle back on the stove for us. Then I peered through the back door, my eyes searching the sky.

'And is Shadow out there too?' I asked, really hoping so for Finn's sake. 'We saw him with Vixen earlier.'

'Oh, sorry, no.' Arlock's chest was rising up and down as if he was struggling to breathe. 'But the little feller's always with us in spirit, if you know what I mean?'

'Oh, erm, yeah, sure,' I lied, shutting the door and carefully avoiding Finn's gaze.

Because I knew what was going through *his* mind right now. Yet more riddles from Arlock. As for me, I was more concerned with getting our visitor some honey and lemon for his chest. I waited until he was gratefully sipping his hot drink before bringing up the children's home again.

'A children's home?' To my astonishment, Arlock seemed to know nothing about it. 'At Dragondah Castle, you say?'

'Yeah, didn't you notice them putting signs up over there at the weekend?'

'Huh, I've been feeling so under the weather these past few days, I wouldn't have noticed if they'd been setting off fireworks at the weekend.' Arlock's gaze was troubled. 'So, you'd best fill me in, Ottillee. First off, when did *you* find out what was going on?'

'Oh, it was in the local paper yesterday.' I sipped my tea. 'And I was really quite shocked, Arlock. I mean, it's up to Finn if he wants to turn the castle into a children's home, isn't it? The council only had to look at King Locryn's bedchamber to know the place *belongs* to someone—'

'Yes, well, I can only imagine they thought squatters had taken up residence there.' Arlock drained his drink before a weary shake of his head. 'So tell me, what well-meaning, but — now, how can I put this politely? — *presumptuous* charity thinks it's perfectly acceptable to take over someone else's ancestral home without their permission?'

'Oh, no, it's not a well-meaning charity, Arlock. It's Lucifer Branson.'

'Lucifer *Branson?*'

'Yeah, you know, the man who was here just now?'

Arlock blinked for several seconds as if he was trying to digest what I'd just said.

'Ye gods, Lucifer *Branson,* is it? And a children's home, of all things. I certainly wasn't expecting that.'

'Yeah, you know him from somewhere, right? I could tell you didn't like him much. I mean, how can a big bully like

Lucifer Branson get permission to open a children's home, hey? Even if he has got loads of money? Oh, are you okay?'

This as Arlock had suddenly gone into some sort of trance. His mouth was half-open, his head was tilted to one side, and his eyes were fixed upon the ceiling.

'Arlock? Wake up, will you?' I urged after several worrying seconds. 'Wake up, *please!* Finn, go and get him some water.'

But it was only when a concerned Vixen nuzzled Arlock with her cold nose that he returned to his senses. His eyes flickered for a few seconds before they were able to focus on mine.

'Sorry about that, Ottillee. I've just had the strangest feeling. Almost as though The Dragon—' he shook his head, as if impatient with himself. 'Oh, take no notice of my ramblings, child. Your news about Lucifer Branson and the castle — well, it quite threw me, I'm afraid.'

'Yes, the last thing we need is a shifty stinker like him sticking his nose in round here, isn't it? And I'm so sorry to have dropped it on you like that.'

And I *was* sorry. My thoughtless announcement had brought on Arlock's funny turn. And when he accepted the glass of water with shaking hands, my heart went out to him.

'Why don't you go and have a lie down for a few minutes?' I suggested. 'There's a nice big couch in our living room.

Or you can go the quick way home, if you like? The tunnel would be so much faster for you than the woods—'

'NEVER will I set foot in there!' Arlock exploded, his breath rattling alarmingly in his chest. 'Bad enough that illicit enterprise is right on my very own doorstep! Yes, believe me, Ottillee, entering Judas Crow's old home today was a big enough challenge for me as it was!'

I nodded, taken aback by Arlock's vehemence, but realising that the hatred for Dragondah's merciless wreckers and smugglers still ran deep round these parts. Nanna Nessa was just as bitter about them. And now Arlock turned his wrath onto the new development at the castle.'

'And as for this so-called *children's* home—'

'Oh, Arlock, forget about that for now. You've just got to try and get yourself well again. Finn and I can keep an eye on what Lucifer Branson's up to—'

Another explosion.

'No! You two steer well clear of that miserable scavenger! Especially you, Finn. Do exactly what you did today and make yourself scarce whenever he's around.'

'But I did—'

'Oh, Arlock, *please* don't worry.' I shot Finn a warning glance. The last thing poor Arlock needed was further distress. To learn that Finn *hadn't* made himself scarce. And that he'd even been offered a place at this so-called children's home. 'We hate the, erm, "miserable scavenger" even more than you do. So we'll just stick with the plan and spend every waking minute trying to find The Dragondah Chronicles, okay?'

'Make sure you do, Ottillee. Because it's vital we find those castle deeds before Lucifer's plans progress too far.' Arlock rummaged about in his pocket. 'Indeed, it was very remiss of me not to give you this the other day. The crosses show where I've already searched.'

And with this, Arlock produced a well-worn map of Dragondah. As it was already covered with crosses, it seemed Finn and I were being asked to go over old ground, but with fresh eyes.

'And are we looking for some sort of old book, do you think?' I asked. 'Like that fake one Finn's dad put together?'

'Most likely, Ottillee. After all, Cador was one of the few people on earth who'd actually set eyes on The Dragondah Chronicles. Although the real book is sure to be much, much older, and possibly hidden away in some sort of old chest—'

'Like a treasure chest, you mean?'

'If you like, lad.'

Arlock finally managed a smile, and I turned my attention to the map again.

'I see you haven't put a cross over Dragondah Hall, Arlock. Don't you think we should have a good look round here too?'

He shook his head. 'There's no point, child. After all,

this was once a Crow residence, wasn't it? And with all the bad blood between the Crows and the Penhaligons, Dragondah Hall would be the last place The Chronicles would ever be.'

Mmmm, I thought as I watched Finn follow Arlock and Vixen out of the door. I'll be the judge of that.

∞∞∞∞

26

'Of Course I'm Not Scared Of You.'

I'M GOING TO look for The Dragondah Chronicles in the library, I decided. And I'm going to look for them right now. I didn't care Arlock considered it a total waste of time. Something was telling me to search Dragondah Hall from top to bottom. And where better to start than in an old room full of old books? I mean, some of them were *so* old they were practically falling to pieces. And there must have been over a thousand of them in there.

I made my way along the hall, passing door after door and feeling like the *real* mistress of Dragondah Hall for the very first time. What with Mum upstairs and everyone else gone, it was as though I had the whole house to myself for once. But when I peered through the half-open door of the library, I couldn't help wish someone, *anyone*, was standing next to me.

'What — what the heck do you think you're doing?' I stammered, my heart hammering away in my chest. 'I thought you'd left ages ago?'

Lucifer Branson peered down at me from the top rung of the library ladder. From his cool expression, anyone would think he had every right to be leafing through our encyclopedias.

'Oh, Ottillee, I didn't hear you sneak in there,' he countered smoothly before snapping shut a heavy book. 'I thought I'd just have a quick look for Dragondah Hall's architectural plans. I promised your mother I'd get someone to help with the outdated wiring, and you know how—'

Lucifer Branson was going on and on now, but I'd stopped listening after 'outdated wiring'. The man was obviously lying through his teeth. Whatever he was up to in our library, it had nothing to do with our electricity. I watched him carefully negotiate his way down the ladder, hoping his lizard-skin shoes were as slippery as everything else about him. Sadly, they weren't, and he got to the bottom safely.

'Mum's only upstairs, you know,' I said tightly when he started striding across the carpet towards me. 'Maybe you could discuss the outdated wiring with her?'

'Maybe I could, Ottillee.' Lucifer Branson's teeth flashed white as he came to a halt in front of me. 'But why are you hovering in the doorway like this? You're not *scared* of me, are you?'

'Of course I'm not scared of you,' I lied, drawing myself up to my full height and trying to ignore the lurch in my chest when Lucifer Branson still managed to tower over me. 'Why the heck would I be?'

'Oh, I don't know.' A lazy smile was playing about his lips. 'Maybe because you've noticed how much your mother enjoys my company? Maybe because you're worried I might take the place of your father one day?'

I gasped at his conceit. 'You could never in a million years take the place of my father,' I hissed. 'My father is — *was* a hero, and my mum loved him more than anyone else in the world. While *you*, you're nothing but a—'

'Nothing but a *what?*' Lucifer Branson smiled at my hesitation. He folded his arms across his chest and considered me through his one good eye. 'You seem to have taken against me astonishingly quickly, young lady. Or maybe it's that sorry excuse for a man who poisoned your mind against me?'

'Who — who do you mean?'

'Oh, don't play the innocent with me. You know *exactly* who I mean. That shady character who wandered into your kitchen just now.' Lucifer Branson's eye narrowed

even further. 'What was his name again? Armlock, was it? Or something equally ridiculous—'

'Arlock,' I corrected without thinking.

'Mmmm, Arlock, is it?' He nodded thoughtfully. 'Something tells me *Arlock* isn't my biggest fan, which is strange considering our paths have never even crossed before. Do you think he's got something against handsome philanthropists with more money than they know what to do with?'

I rolled my eyes at such an arrogant suggestion. How I'd have loved to list all the reasons why Arlock disliked Lucifer Branson so much. But I'd no idea — Arlock had warned us against him even *before* he'd learnt of his plans for the castle. Although it didn't take long for our visitor to come up with a reason of his own, of course.

'Oh, I get it, Ottillee. Arlock's a rival for your mother's affections, isn't he?' He was openly taunting me now. 'I'll admit he might be *some* women's idea of a romantic hero. That's if he ever bothered to shave or brush—'

'Oh, you, why do you always have to twist everything? Arlock's never even *met* my mum before this morning. It was me who asked him to come today. To help with our

outdated wiring, if you must know.' It was obvious I was lying, but I didn't care a jot. 'So you can leave now, if you don't mind—'

I stepped further into the library, silently inviting Lucifer Branson to walk past me and leave Dragondah Hall for good. But much to my alarm, he reached out his hand and slammed the door shut behind me.

My insides lurched at the realisation that I was trapped in a room with the man Arlock had so recently warned us against. Lucifer Branson's face was now so close to mine that I could smell what he'd had for breakfast. (And I hated kippers with a passion.) But I stood my ground, not just to hide my fear but because I was suddenly hypnotised by the tiny symbol in the middle of his eye patch.

And that was because I'd finally worked out what it was supposed to represent. A bird's outstretched wing. Now, why the heck would—?

'You should be with me, not against me, young lady.' Lucifer Branson's words broke through my frantic thoughts, the threat evident in his tone. 'Your life here in Dragondah would be so much easier. You know, what with your dad being, erm, as dead as a dodo, and all that.'

Lucifer Branson knew exactly how to hurt me the most. I did my best not to react, but my dismay must have shown on my face because he laughed at me. Then before I knew it, he was lifting his eye patch and I was rushing to cover my face. Like a lily-livered coward, I knew, but when I finally summoned up the courage to look, my instant response wasn't a gasp of sympathy but a cry of horror. Because two cold, calculating and perfectly healthy eyes were glaring back at me. Lucifer Branson's eye patch was as false as everything else about him.

'You're way out of your depth, Ottillee,' he said as he snapped the eye patch back in place. 'You're nothing but a precocious little schoolgirl, and I'll always be one step ahead of you.'

I had no answer to that, my mind still grappling with what had just happened. Just when I thought Lucifer Branson couldn't get any worse, he did. Only this time even *he* seemed to realise he'd gone too far.

'Although I'm nowhere near as bad as you appear to think I am, young lady.' His lofty sneer suddenly transformed into a charming smile. 'Why don't you let me prove it to you?'

'Huh! *How?*'

'I'm driving your mother over to the castle tomorrow and giving her a bit of a tour.'

'You *are?*'

'Yes, so why don't you and Finn come along too? I'd love to share the plans for my new children's academy with you.'

'We'd rather stick pins in our—'

'Yes, we could easily pick up Finn on the way,' he interrupted smoothly. 'He doesn't live *that* far from the lane.'

'How — how do *you* know where Finn lives?'

'Oh, it's surprising what you can see from a helicopter when you look hard enough, Ottillee. Even a broken-down old lorry sheltering beneath a tree.' A sad little shake of his head. 'I must say Finn's living conditions leave quite a lot to be desired, don't they? If only the poor boy would let me help him.'

Huh! I wasn't falling for Lucifer Branson's sudden show of concern. All he wanted was to get his children's home up and running. Or his *so-called* children's home as Arlock had called it, clearly suspecting it was some sort of ruse. Yes, maybe it wouldn't hurt to get to the bottom of what Lucifer Branson was *really* up to at the castle? With a bit of luck, he might even reveal his true colours to Mum.

'Come on, Ottillee, most kids would enjoy a personal tour of a medieval castle.' He could see I was wavering. 'Anyone would think you and Finn were scared!'

'Of course we're not scared.' I knew what tactics Lucifer

Branson was using but I could never resist a challenge. 'We — we will come to the castle if it's so important to you.'

'You promise?'

'I promise.'

'Good girl.' A satisfied Lucifer Branson patted me on the shoulder as he left the library. But I didn't start breathing again until I heard his jeep zooming off down the driveway, and the speckled crow — sorry, *raven* — squawking with delight.

———◦◦◇◇◦◦———

Dad's Secret Report

DATE: Wednesday, 15 August, 2018   TIME: Middle of the night
PLACE: You know.   SUBJECT: Big mistake?

Dear Dad,

I've been tossing and turning for five whole hours now, but I still can't fall asleep. Why is it that everything always feels so much worse in the middle of the night?

I mean, Lucifer Branson's even shiftier and stinkier than I imagined. And he <u>still</u> thinks he's in with a chance of marrying your very own wife, GRACE BOTTOMLY. Huh! As if Mum would ever <u>look</u> at another man, let alone kiss him at the altar. (Or any other place, come to that.) Although I will admit that Mum does seem to think of Lucifer Branson as a kind and helpful friend. You know, the sort of person to go on jaunts with and enjoy hot beverages with, his handyman skills clearly an added bonus. I mean, she'd never believe he said hurtful things behind her back or that his eye patch was a total fake. And if I told her Arlock had warned us to stay well away from him, she'd probably just smile and say there are always two sides to every story. AAAAARGH!!

Anyway, I've <u>reluctantly</u> agreed to go over to the castle with Lucifer Branson and Mum tomorrow. Arlock won't be happy about it (especially as I've agreed for Finn to come along too), but nothing bad can happen to any of us in broad daylight, can it? And the hunt for The Dragondah Chronicles can wait one more day surely? I just thought this was our best chance of finding out exactly what's going on over there. And if we get lucky, maybe Lucifer Branson will let his mask (or his eye patch) slip and show Mum the kind of man he <u>really</u> is. A big bully who doesn't give a fig for Cornish orphans, Cornish history or Cornish wildlife — despite what The Cornish Clarion newspaper said. Then at least, Mum will stop letting him through the front door. And get someone else to do her household maintenance jobs.

Wish us luck, Dad.
Your loving...

Oh, poop! I couldn't remember the Cornish word for 'daughter'. With a weary sigh, I put down my pen and paper and picked up the Cornish/English dictionary on my bedside table.

It was still open at ENEVALES HA EDHNOW (or ANIMALS AND BIRDS for the non-Cornish-speakers), and I rolled my eyes at the confusing jumble of letters. Honestly, Cornish was really starting to get on my last nerve now. Would you believe 'dh' was pronounced 'th', for example? And 'hw' was pronounced 'wh'? Who thought *that* was a good idea? I mean, it was even worse than French.

Then suddenly, my tired eyes fell upon a simple Cornish word that even *I* knew how to pronounce. In fact, the four letters were practically jumping off the page at me. But it was only when I looked across at the English translation that I shot upright, my heart pumping away in my chest as if I'd had an electric shock.

No, surely not? I thought, as appalled as I was stunned.

Surely no one in the world could be that devious, could they? That vengeful? But then, as I fell back against my pillows and my frantic brain started sifting through the strange events, conversations and hostilities of the past few weeks, I changed that to a big fat *yes of course they could!* It was the only thing that made any sense.

Problem was, what was I going to do about it? I'd already promised that Finn and I would go to Dragondah Castle tomorrow. Pulling out of the trip at the last minute would only make Lucifer Branson suspicious. As for telling Mum about my discovery, she'd just say I was allowing hatred to cloud my judgement and seeing things that weren't there. No, it was best the arrangements stayed as they were for now. As I'd just reassured Dad, nothing bad could happen to any of us in broad daylight, could it?

28

'Hush, Finn!'

'OH, MY GIDDY AUNT!' Mum shrieked as Dagger raced eighty miles per hour across the empty beach towards Dragondah Island. Our vehicle was more like a tank than a jeep, and I couldn't help fear for any creatures unlucky enough to get in our way that morning. Sand, seawater and seagulls were flying off in all directions.

'Everyone enjoying themselves?' asked a beaming Lucifer Branson who was clearly having a whale of a time in the passenger seat.

Mum, Finn and I were seated behind wearing strained expressions on our faces. Mum wasn't a good passenger at the best of times. Finn was brooding because Shadow had gone missing again. (Oh yes, and because 'some skogyn' had dragged him off on this last-minute day trip with the local bully.) As for the 'skogyn' herself, I simply refused to smile whenever Lucifer Branson was smiling. Instead, I was simmering away quietly, needing all my self-restraint not to twang his fake eye patch, never mind blurt out his other shocking secret.

At least the journey to the castle was completed in record time. Dagger let us out by the eastern wall before scuttling off to 'check his traps'. I couldn't help feel sorry for the poor rat, especially as Dagger had turned out to be a little rat of a man himself now that we could see him properly. His eyes were beady, his nose was pink, and his chin was nowhere to be seen. He also appeared to be dressed for big game hunting this morning, his socks and sandals teamed with khaki shorts so big and baggy that they swamped his slight frame.

As for Lucifer Branson, he was on his best behaviour and only concerned with the welfare of his guests.

'Yes, Ottillee, they're almost jewel-like in colour, aren't they?' he commented rather poetically when he spotted me gazing at some dragonflies darting about a rock pool. 'Dragondah Island is quite the nature reserve, isn't it?'

'Suppose so,' I muttered back rather *less* poetically, only for him to give up on me and turn his attention to Finn instead.

'And what about you, young man? Did you enjoy the drive?' Lucifer Branson didn't let Finn's careless shrug put him off. 'Of course, that monster jeep will be at the beck and call of all the children in my care.'

'But, Lucifer, what happens when it's high tide?' Mum

asked as she allowed him to lead her up the steps towards the gatehouse. 'Won't the kids be cut off from the mainland every day?'

'Oh, I doubt they'll even notice, Gracey. They'll have everything they could possibly want at the castle.'

Lucifer Branson was talking far louder than was necessary, considering Finn and I were following right behind him. His unashamed sales pitch continued when we made our way into the courtyard.

'And don't forget there's acres of outdoor space here too. In fact, we've got plans for a bridge, so the land beyond the rock pools is always accessible, even at high tide. Now, you tell me what young lad wouldn't love to be able to play on his own wilderness island?'

I released an irritated sigh. Lucifer Branson was *really* pulling out all the stops to make Finn reconsider his academy. Although judging by the grim expression on Finn's face, he wasn't making much progress. In fact, the only person falling for it all hook, line and sinker was Mum. Yes, she was happily asking her questions as we crossed the cobbles, and I was getting more irritated with every bare-faced lie Lucifer Branson told her.

At first, it was all academy stuff. Yes, he'd ensure the waterhole had a safety cover over it. No, he didn't think the orphans would be scared by the statue of the wolf. Yes, of course he'd close off the steep steps to the battlements so no one would have a nasty fall.

But when we moved inside into the Great Hall, the focus was all on him. How visionary he was, how rich he was, and even how generous he was. 'Far too generous for my own good' were Lucifer Branson's *exact* words, his booming voice echoing around the vast empty space. The kids would all get their own rooms, he boasted. They'd dine on the freshest local produce, and they'd be taught by the best teachers in Cornwall. It all sounded so impressive that Mum called him a 'total hero' and asked whether the academy accepted 35-year-old widows? I don't even think she was joking.

'Can we go up the tower too?' And now Mum was pointing towards the stairway in the corner. 'What a treat it would be to get a seagull's eye view over all Dragondah, hey, Ottillee?'

My eyes widened, as did Finn's. How was Lucifer Branson going to explain King Locryn's fully furnished bedchamber on the top floor? But the man was too smart not to have thought that one through already.

'Sorry, Gracey, but it's strictly out-of-bounds up there at the moment.' He crossed the flagstones and made a great fuss of straightening a 'CAUTION — HARD HAT AREA!' sign before smiling apologetically. 'These steps are a death trap, and I can't allow anyone near them until they've been reinforced.'

'Huh!' I heard Finn exclaim a little too loudly. 'You're not the king of the castle *yet*, you know.'

'Hush, Finn!' I hissed urgently, but Lucifer Branson had already heard him.

'What was that, lad?' he asked with a pleasant smile.

'Just that Ottillee and I went up that tower a few days ago. Those steps seemed perfectly safe to us.'

'What?' Lucifer Branson's pleasant smile vanished. 'You trespassed on *my* castle? And — and you ignored *my* safety signs?'

'Yeah, of course we did.' Finn had clearly had enough of Lucifer Branson's arrogant claims and was directing his words at my mum now. 'And you're right, Mrs Bottomly, the views *are* amazing from up there.'

'Well, really, I can't believe you had the temerity to—'

But Finn took no notice of Lucifer Branson's blustering. Or my own desperate attempts to shut him up. Oh, *why* the heck hadn't I found a way to share my shocking discovery with Finn this morning? Why hadn't I warned him to keep his head down?

'Yes, Mrs Bottomly, there's this amazing four-poster bed up there,' Finn continued as he shook off my restraining hand. 'Almost a thousand years old it is. It once belonged to the great King Locryn Penhaligon, you see—'

'King Locryn Penhaligon?' Mum was taking no notice of my frenzied signals either.

'Yeah, you see the Penhaligons are the *real* owners of this castle, not your Mr Branson here—'

'Finn! Shut up, will you?' I was getting desperate. 'Trust me, this isn't the time!'

But my warnings had come too late. Lucifer Branson's sudden transformation from charming host to spitting adversary was frightening.

'What drivel you're talking, boy!' he bellowed. 'The Penhaligons had as much right to this castle as they did to the Cornish monarchy! No right at all! Those rogues *stole* this land just as they did the throne itself. Helped themselves to it all like common criminals!'

Even I'd not expected such fury. Yes, I'd wanted Lucifer Branson to reveal his true colours, but that was before I knew what his true colours *were*. Mum was looking shocked to the core too.

'Oh, Lucifer, I'm sure the boy didn't mean to upset you,' she said soothingly while putting her arm around Finn's shoulders. 'He'll have just read about that old king somewhere. You know how these legendary figures get exaggerated over the years—'

'But King Locryn wasn't a legendary figure, Mrs Bottomly. He was a real king, and he was my—'

'NO, FINN! DON'T SAY ANOTHER WORD!'

I was quite frantic now. Lucifer Branson had already lost control at the very *mention* of the Penhaligons. What would he do if he discovered Finn was a Penhaligon himself? And then things went from bad to worse. A triumphant shout could be heard as Dagger dashed into the Great Hall clutching a bundle of netting. Dagger had finally caught his rat, and from the desperate squeals and the way the net was jerking about, the poor creature was still very much alive.

'Gave me the right run-around, it did, sir,' the delighted man cried as he came to a halt in front of his boss. 'Nearly bit my thumb off, can you believe? Got it in the end though, didn't I!'

'At last!' Lucifer Branson poked the living captive before turning to my startled mother. 'You'll hardly believe it, Gracey, but this little pest could have put an end to all my plans.'

'Yes, Mrs Bottomly, it was *me* who thought of putting a very fine net over the rock pools at the other end of the island.' Dagger clearly wanted to get the credit due to him. 'One smart little blighter this one is, but even smart little blighters need a drink of water sometimes.'

'Yes, well, I hope it enjoyed its drink because it's the last one it's ever going to get.'

Lucifer Branson smiled cruelly, and Finn and I exchanged horrified glances. There was clearly no happy ending in sight for the castle's resident rat, and Mum was looking just as concerned.

'Honestly, Lucifer, what a fuss you're making over some poor, harmless creature.' She stepped closer to Dagger to get a better look. 'What on earth have you got there?'

And then there was a rapid fluttering of leathery black wings, and it was obvious what Dagger had got there. He'd got Shadow.

———⬥◇◇◇◇⬥———

29

'Give Him What For!'

FINN WAS on Dagger in the blink of an eye. He desperately tried to wrestle the net away, but Dagger was too strong. Even when I pitched in seconds later, Dagger put up a surprisingly good fight for such a slight man. And then it was Mum's turn to get involved.

'Ottillee! You must *never* resort to violence!' she cried, dragging me away from the scuffle at no little risk to herself. 'Hey, what are you doing, Lucifer?'

This as Lucifer Branson was resorting to violence himself. Mum and I watched with horror as he got Finn in a headlock before tossing him to the floor. Yet a cussing Finn still had plenty of fight left in him. Crawling across the flagstones, he attempted to reach Shadow from beneath, but Dagger held the net high above his head.

Then, while Lucifer Branson restrained Finn, Dagger tied a knot around the struggling bundle and placed it well out of reach on one of the hall's deep window ledges.

Shadow's frustrated squeaks and flailing wings were almost breaking my heart, so I could imagine the effect they were having on Finn. And then I didn't have to imagine any longer. Finn twisted out of Lucifer Branson's grasp and glared at him with undisguised fury.

'My name is Finn Penhaligon!' he declared with all the bitter arrogance of a long-lost Cornish king. 'I *own* this castle, and I'm ordering you to let my flittermouse go!'

I was rooted to the spot, so proud of my friend's courage, yet also terrified by it. Now that Finn's identity was out in the open, who knew what would happen next, all the way out here, miles away from anyone? But if I was expecting shock and outrage from Lucifer Branson, I was wrong.

'I might have known that flea-ridden creature would have something to do with you, lad,' was his only response. 'Vermin attracts vermin, after all.'

'Oh, no!' My hands flew to my mouth in shocked dismay. *Lucifer Branson had known who Finn was all along!*

Mum was as distraught as I was, wincing up at Shadow whose squeals were getting louder by the second.

'Oh, really, Lucifer, I must insist you release that poor creature up there,' she said. 'I've no idea whether Finn's claims are true, but I do know he's a wonderful young man and neither flea-ridden nor vermin.'

'Oh, *all* Penhaligons are vermin, Gracey. You've only got to look at them.' Lucifer Branson turned to Finn. 'Yes, lad, finally got a *proper* look at you at the Bottomly's little tea party yesterday, didn't I? And just as I'd long suspected, you're Cador's boy all right. All the family traits are there. The white skin, the black hair, the cleft in the chin and, of course, those accursed Penhaligon eyes—'

'*Accursed* Penhaligon eyes?' A horrified Finn swung round to me. 'But — but why would he say something like that, Ottillee? And how the heck does he know all this stuff about my family anyway?'

'Oh, I'll tell you *exactly* how he knows.' My own gaze remained fixed upon Lucifer Branson, my breathing fast, my thoughts churning. There was no doubt the man had outplayed us. And now, there was only one card left to play. Just as Finn's real identity was out in the open, it was time for our enemy's real identity to be out in the open too. 'And if you just think about Lucifer's surname for a second, Finn — or rather his *fake* surname — you'll work it out for yourself.'

'His *fake* surname?' A puzzled Finn met my gaze. 'Branson, you mean?'

'Yes, because what does the word "bran" mean in Cornish?'

'Bran?' Finn looked even more confused. 'I can't remember—'

'Come on, Finn,' I urged. '*Try.*'

'It means—' Finn was clearly racking his brains, 'it

means some sort of bird. Erm, a crow, yes, a crow, I think.'

'Exactly!'

There was silence for the briefest of moments. Even Shadow had been stunned into silence up there on his window ledge. And then Finn hit his head with the heel of his hand.

'Cripes, Ottillee! Why didn't I think of it before? "Bran" means crow, so "Bran-son" means son of a crow!'

'Exactly. Lucifer Branson is really Judas Crow's son!' I glowered at Lucifer Branson — or rather Lucifer *Crow* — just as Mum was doing. 'You must have thought you were so clever fooling us all like that?'

'I've no idea what you're on about, Ottillee.' And now the imposter was pretending to clean the dirt from under his fingernails. 'In fact, aren't you getting a little desperate?'

'No, it's *you* who's the desperate one. It's you who — it's you who—' the enormity of what I was doing was suddenly hitting me. But then Mum took hold of my right hand and Finn took hold of my left, and their support gave me the courage to continue. 'Yes, it's *you* who had to use a false name, because everyone in Cornwall hates your family—'

'What tosh!'

'Yes, and it's *you* who had to wear a fake eye patch to make yourself look like a hero—'

'I'll have you know that I lost my left eye in a fire—'

'Oh, pull the other one! You know there's nothing wrong

with your left eye! But you couldn't resist flaunting your *real* name in all our faces, could you? Because there it is, right in the middle of your eye patch — a crow's wing!'

More shocked gasps from Mum and Finn, but I wasn't finished yet.

'Yeah, I never trusted you, you big phoney. At first, I thought you were just after my mum—'

'Oh, really, sweetheart—'

I ignored Mum. 'And then I realised you were after the castle too. But right up until last night, I *thought* you were just some rich bully wanting to push poor kids around. I never realised you only wanted to push Finn Penhaligon around—'

Silence fell over the Great Hall, no one sure what was going to happen next, including me. Shadow's netting had also gone worryingly still. And then, to my astonishment, Lucifer Crow grinned and gave me a round of applause.

'Bravo, Ottillee, it seems I underestimated you. Although you did get one thing wrong. I didn't want to push Finn Penhaligon *around*. I wanted to push him down that very deep waterhole in the castle courtyard!'

More shocked cries from Mum and Finn. Dagger was horrified too, but for a different reason.

'Oh, sir, why did you have to go and admit *that?*' he groaned. 'You've ruined everything now. And with your father hardly cold in his grave—'

'Oh, Judas has only got himself to blame, Dagger. If he'd found out about Cador's death ten years earlier, Finn would still be an infant in the crib instead of some skinny youth with an attitude.' Lucifer Crow turned to smile at me now. 'As would you, Ottillee. And Dragondah Castle would already be mine.'

'Yes, well, Dragondah Castle isn't yours, is it?' I hissed. 'It's Finn's—'

'Maybe, but the boy will never be able to prove it—'

'Oh, yes, he will.'

'Oh, no, he won't. And all it took for me to confirm this happy state of affairs was a search of your library—'

'Oh, I *knew* you were up to something on that ladder!'

'Right again, Ottillee. I was looking for an old wooden chest with a particularly distinctive dragon clasp on the front of it.' Lucifer Crow's smile was now taking in both me and Finn. 'Does that sound familiar to either of you?'

'Oh, no!' I cried. 'You're not talking about The Dragondah—?'

'Chronicles? Yes, I *am!*' Lucifer Crow laughed at my panic-stricken expression. 'And who'd ever have thought the Penhaligon's most precious possession would be secreted away on the top shelf of the Crow's library, hey? Or rather that's where it *was* until Cowenna spotted Judas trying to open the accursed casket and moved it double-quick—'

'Good for her!' I cried, trying to hide my shock that The Chronicles had ever been kept at Dragondah Hall. Even eighty years ago.

'Yes, I was just checking the traitorous old witch hadn't moved The Chronicles back again. Who knows? Maybe she felt it was safe once Judas had left her and married my mother. Or maybe Cador himself had returned the chest to the library, knowing it was the last place anyone would look.'

'Yeah, well, the chest wasn't in the library, was it? And that's because it's somewhere else entirely.' I was bluffing now. 'And Cowenna told me exactly where that was—'

'Oh, no, she didn't.' Lucifer Crow smirked at me. 'Cowenna told you nothing about her past—'

'Oh, yes she did—'

'Oh, no, she didn't! Because otherwise, you and that Penhaligon waste-of-space over there would be wafting the castle deeds in my face. And I'd have been kicked out of Dragondah long ago!'

'But—'

'Oh, stop bluffing, Ottillee. Just count yourself lucky I never kicked *you* out of Dragondah Hall.'

'What?'

'Yes, you're forgetting the Crows built that house you're swanning about in. It was their home for over three hundred years—'

'But it's *our* home now,' Mum cried in shocked dismay.

'Oh, don't worry, Gracey.' Despite everything, Lucifer Crow still had a soft spot for Mum. 'As much as it pains me to admit it, my father lost Dragondah Hall in a card game to Cowenna. Signed the place over to her lock, stock and barrel on their wedding day, more fool him.'

'Oh, thank heavens!'

'Yes, Gracey, people can say what they like about Judas Crow but he always paid his gambling debts. Even to a conniving young woman like Cowenna Penhaligon.'

'How dare you call Cowenna "conniving",' I cried furiously. 'She was just looking out for herself—'

'Never a truer word was said, Ottillee. Because she wasn't looking out for anyone else, was she?' He smiled cruelly. 'No wonder she left you everything in her will.'

'What do you mean?'

'I mean that you, young lady, are the perfect revenge!'

'The perfect *revenge?*'

'Yes, revenge against the Crows *and* the Penhaligons!'

'But I don't understand. I can't—'

'Well, think about it, you stupid girl. Both families abandoned Cowenna in the end, didn't they?' And now Lucifer Crow was openly sneering at me. 'She was hardly likely to leave all her worldly goods to *any* of them, was she? No, she was much more likely to leave them to some random, snivelling blow-in instead—'

'Oh, don't listen to him, sweetheart.' Mum hugged me to her. 'And Lucifer, I'll ask you to mind what you say to my daughter.'

But Lucifer Crow was turning his venom on Finn now.

'And as for your precious Dragondah Chronicles, boy, their precise location died with Cowenna, didn't it? Or at least with your father Cador. Come on, tell me I'm not right? Tell me you've got more chance of finding the Dragondah dragon than The Dragondah Chronicles! Tell me your castle's not mine for the taking?'

But Finn didn't respond, his eyes fixed upon something high up in the corner of the Great Hall. This only encouraged more venom to drip from Lucifer Crow's mouth.

'Honestly, Dagger, it's hard to believe the Penhaligon dynasty could have ended up in a skinny little runt like this one, isn't it? I don't know why I listened to my father. The boy's hardly *king* material, is he? Why, he can't even fight his own battles without the help of a girl — ouch, what was that?'

This as Lucifer Crow's eye patch flew off, its elastic band bitten in two. And now he was being bombarded from the air by none other than Shadow! While we'd all been arguing, the clever creature had escaped from his net and was now in full attack mode!

'I knew you could do it, my little beauty!' shouted Finn.

'Yes, give him what for!' This from me, although the bat certainly needed no encouragement.

Shadow was putting on an aeronautical display beyond compare this morning, as indignant as he was enraged at being trapped in a net. Wings pulled back like a jet fighter, he was swooping at Lucifer Crow and Dagger, baring his fangs and snapping mercilessly at their heads and backs. He only stopped his onslaught when the two shell-shocked men were cowering on the flagstones and begging for mercy. Then Shadow performed one last victory roll before zooming twice around the Great Hall and out through the door.

Mum, Finn and I weren't long behind him, of course. We raced outside and back down the castle steps towards the beach, all the while congratulating ourselves on a job well done. Even the screeches from the seagulls sounded triumphant to our ears. But our victory was short-lived, lasting only until we'd stepped down onto the sands.

'You might think you've won today,' came the cry from the gatehouse, 'but like it or not, Dragondah Castle is still mine to do with as I like.'

And do you know what? Until we'd found The Dragondah Chronicles, Lucifer Crow was absolutely right.

30

'It's Important, Mum.'

'I HATE TO admit it, Finn, but Lucifer Crow *is* absolutely right. We *have* got more chance of finding the blasted Dragondah dragon than the blasted Dragondah Chronicles!'

I ignored Mum's glare of disapproval (for saying 'blasted' twice) and handed Finn another slice of pizza. I was tucking into my third slice now, always famished whenever I was rattled. Or bone-weary. Or troubled to the very depths of my soul. I mean, for Lucifer Crow to call Finn a 'skinny little runt' was one thing. For him to call *me* the 'perfect revenge' was something else entirely.

It was now six days since our shocking confrontation at Dragondah Castle. Six days that Finn, Mum and I had spent searching everywhere we could think of for proof that Finn was the castle's rightful owner. We'd been under Dragondah Hall's beds, on top of its wardrobes, inside its cupboards and through its bookshelves. We'd also been scratched by Dragondah's brambles, stung by its nettles, bogged down in its ditches and cawed at by its resident crows and ravens. All with no sign of the distinctive wooden chest. It didn't help that Lucifer Crow had been spurred into action too. Nanna Nessa had spotted a lorry-load of men speeding over to the castle yesterday, and I was really starting to fear for King Locryn's bed.

Other stuff was worrying me too. No one had set eyes on Shadow since he'd escaped from Dagger's clutches. And although we'd stopped by the cavern every single day this week, there had been no sign of Arlock either. I was just hoping they'd both taken themselves off somewhere quiet, Shadow to recover from his ordeal and Arlock to recuperate from his illness. Anything else was just too upsetting to think about. And then Finn's frustrated voice broke through my thoughts.

'Honestly, Ottillee, I still can't believe Nan didn't warn me that one of the Crows was back in Dragondah.' He released a world-weary sigh. 'I thought she'd learnt her lesson by now. Why does she still insist on treating me like a kid?'

Mum plonked herself down opposite us with a cup of tea.

'Maybe because you still *are* a kid, Finn,' she said firmly. 'And maybe because she was doing her best to shield you from a very dangerous individual.'

'Yeah, and to be fair, Finn, you never actually *told* your

nan that we'd ever met Lucifer Crow, did you?' I wiped tomato sauce off my chin. 'And don't forget she did warn us about trusting strangers—'

'Yeah, but *I* thought she was talking about — well, you know, someone else.'

'Arlock, you mean?' I rolled my eyes. 'Honestly, Finn, surely you realise by now that you can trust Arlock with your life? I mean, *he* certainly warned us against Lucifer Crow when he saw him in our kitchen, didn't he? Couldn't have been clearer actually—'

'Oh, yes, he could! Arlock *still* let us think Lucifer's last name was Branson. And going on about "scavengers" like he did was hardly clear, was it?'

'Well, crows do scavenge for food, you know—'

'I *know* they do, Ottillee, but I'm not a mind-reader!' Finn shoved his uneaten pizza aside and turned to Mum. 'One of the worst things about all this, Mrs Bottomly, is that everyone else round here still thinks Lucifer Crow's some kind of saint.'

'You're not wrong there, Finn. That police inspector in Bodmin thought I was making it up about him using a false name. Councillor Penrose wouldn't hear a bad word said against him either.' Mum put on a deep manly voice. 'Oh no, Mrs Bottomly, you've got Lucifer mixed up with someone else. A man like that wouldn't harm a fly, let alone an orphan.'

'I know, Mum,' I said. 'It's enough to make you spit.'

I mean, even she'd been taken in by Lucifer Crow at first. Not that I was giving her a hard time about it because she felt bad enough already. And anyway, she'd changed her mind in the end, saying she'd have done it much earlier had I not kept so many secrets from her. Finn and I had filled Mum in on quite a lot of stuff on the walk back from the castle, including everything we knew about the Crows and the Penhaligons.

'We've simply *got* to find those Dragondah Chronicles,' I said now, nibbling dejectedly on my pizza crust. 'If only Arlock were here to help us.'

Finn snorted, and Mum nearly choked on her tea.

'Oh, Ottillee, Arlock can hardly help himself right now!' she scoffed. 'I don't like to be mean, sweetheart, but the poor man's not in the best of health, is he?'

'Yes, well, you *are* being mean, Mum. Actually, I was going to ask if Arlock could come and stay with us here at Dragondah Hall? At least until he gets better. I mean, we've got plenty of bedrooms, haven't we? And it's not doing him any good at all sleeping in that cold, damp cave—'

'What?' Mum slopped her tea in her saucer. 'You're telling me Arlock sleeps in a *cave?*'

Ooops, I'd forgotten I'd not filled her in on absolutely everything that was going on in Dragondah yet.

'Yeah, Arlock's a tramp — I mean a *rough sleeper*. You know, like Bumstead Billy.' I eyed Finn's uneaten slice of pizza. 'But he's a Cornish rough sleeper, so instead of sleeping in the doorway of the cake shop like Billy, he sleeps in, erm — a cave.'

'Honestly, Ottillee, you've clearly been keeping a lot more stuff from me than I realised.' Mum slapped my hand away from Finn's unwanted pizza. 'Anything else you'd like to confess?'

'Of course not,' I replied quickly, but then I had a sudden thought. 'Although—'

'Although *what?*'

'Although you should probably know there's a tunnel leading from our kitchen pantry all the way to the beach.'

'Bless my soul! Surely you're joking?'

'No, the Crow family dug it out so they could move their smuggled booty about in secret. Judas Crow probably used it all the time.'

'Oh, that *damn* Judas Crow!' Mum rarely swore in front of me. 'If only I hadn't let his scheming son into this house. Honestly, Ottillee, your father would have seen right through Lucifer the moment he clapped eyes on him.'

'Yeah, he most certainly would,' I muttered grimly. Now wasn't the time to remind Mum that *I'd* seen through Lucifer the moment I'd clapped eyes on him. 'He wouldn't have been quite so full of himself, that's for sure.'

'Yeah, that man's got more sauce than a Stargazey pie.' This from Finn as he dragged himself to his feet. 'Anyway, I'm sick of talking about the Crows. Come on, Ottillee, let's go and look for Shadow again. I'm worried sick about him.'

But I stayed where I was. Because I was thinking about six days ago when Lucifer Crow *hadn't* got more sauce than a so-called Stargazey pie. When he'd been so worried about a bat flying around Dragondah Castle that he'd tried to have it killed. And what the heck had he meant when he'd said Shadow could put an end to all his plans? Suddenly, I had an idea.

'Hey, Mum, you couldn't drive us into the village, could you? There's something I want to look up on the internet.'

'But I'd rather go and look for Shadow again, Ottillee.'

I ignored Finn. 'Will you take us, Mum?'

'Oh, I don't know, sweetheart. Chuggypig's a bit of a drive and I've got to make the meal—'

'It's important, Mum, *really* important.'

Mum held my gaze for a long moment and then, much to my relief, she nodded. Thirty minutes later, the three of us were sat around a table in the otherwise empty Chuggypig Café with three unwanted drinks in front of us.

I wasted no time typing Lucifer Branson's name onto the keyboard of Mum's tablet. Finn was looking on in bemusement, although whether this was because of my super-duper typing skills or because he'd never used the internet before, I didn't ask. I was concentrating on the screen and wondering how many murky secrets we were about to uncover.

But nothing except the recent *Cornish Clarion* article about The Dragondah Castle Children's Academy came up. I scowled at the screen for a few seconds, only to tut at my stupidity. This time I typed Lucifer *Crow* into the search engine and got much better results.

'I don't believe it,' I breathed as I skimmed through a story that had appeared in a paper called *The Scilly Standard* about three years ago. (Who knew the Scilly Islands were a real place, after all?) 'Now, listen to this, everyone—'

But it was Finn who started reading over my shoulder, racing through the article at a rate of knots.

'Lucifer Crow's dreams for Cadwallader Castle lay in tatters today. Questions are being asked whether the mysterious businessman can ever recover from such a huge financial setback. Yet the local council insists they had no choice but to pull the plug on Crow's new company headquarters, thereby losing him millions of pounds in construction charges. They also felt morally obliged to fine him a record £20,000 for his crimes against bats—'

'Crimes against bats?' interjected Mum. 'I didn't know there was such a thing? And why is Lucifer so obsessed with old castles anyway?'

But Finn just kept on reading.

'It is illegal to harm, kill, capture or even disturb bats in the UK. Lucifer Crow's long list of crimes includes failure to carry out a bat survey, flying a helicopter too close to a bat, killing an entire colony of bats and illegally destroying a bat roost that has been there for centuries—'

'Well, that explains a lot,' said Mum.

'Yes, and there's more.' Finn scrolled further down the article with my help.

'"We will not tolerate bat crime," said a representative for BUTT (Bats Under Terrible Threat). "Bats are crucial to the ecosystem of the entire UK and, unfortunately for Mr Crow, this includes uninhabited islands in the Scilly Islands. Bats pollinate plants, disperse seeds, help with forest regrowth, clear the air of blood-sucking mosquitoes and even reduce the need for pesticides. Their roosting sites, whether occupied or not, are protected by the full force of the law—"'

'Who knew?'

'Shush, Mum! Let Finn finish.'

'"Hopefully, Mr Crow has now learnt his lesson, and will ensure these exceptional creatures are not only given the space they need but also the respect they deserve."'

Finn released a heavy sigh, his gaze bleak when it met mine. 'You know what this means, don't you?' he said darkly. 'That Shadow was lucky to get away with his life the other day. That's if he even did—'

'Oh, of course he did!' I hastened to tell Finn what *good* news this was. Not for the poor Scilly Island bats, of course, but for us and for Shadow too, fingers crossed.

Because surely BUTT (Bats Under Terrible Threat) would be most interested to learn that Lucifer Crow was *still* capturing bats and threatening them with death here in Dragondah? And surely Councillor Penrose, or whatever his name was, would be forced to pull the plug on the castle development once the papers got hold of the story? Mum and Finn could hardly contain themselves by the time I'd finished explaining.

'So, erm, so erm, so what should we do now then, Ottillee?' Finn was so excited he could hardly get his words out. 'Contact these BUTT people? Or the local council again? Or even *The Cornish Clarion*?'

'Oh, I think the *first* thing we should do is find Shadow. I mean, without him, we don't really have a leg to stand on, do we?'

'You're right, sweetheart.' Mum drained her tea and got to her feet. 'And then I think you should bring the poor little soul back to us for safekeeping. After all, we don't want that dirty scumbag Lucifer Crow getting his mitts on him again, do we?'

'Too right!' I said with an approving nod. As trusting as she was, Mum clearly didn't take kindly to being played for a fool.

'Any idea where Shadow might be hiding out?' she asked as we left the café and hurried to the car.

'Not really.' I tossed Finn a worried glance. 'He's been keeping a very low profile since he was captured in that net, hasn't he?'

'Yeah, but this time we're not giving up until we've tracked him down.' Finn's mouth tightened. 'Come on, Ottillee, we're going bat hunting. Let's try Arlock's cavern first.'

31

'Are You Okay, Arlock?'

MINUTES LATER, Finn and I were racing along the secret tunnel. What a relief it was to know that the missing Dragondah Chronicles could *stay* missing for now. That a stroppy little bat was all that was needed to get Lucifer Crow kicked out of Dragondah Castle! But when we reached the cavern, it was to find there was no one there. No Shadow, no Arlock, no Vixen. Just the glow from that unsettling beam of light. Exactly like it had been these past six days.

'Okay, Finn, let's go over to your place now,' I puffed, already heading for the beach. 'Maybe Shadow's finally gone back home—'

'Hey, Ottillee, shush for a second, will you? Can you hear something?'

And, yes, I most certainly could. Gentle snores were coming from behind one of the boulders. Finn and I dashed over to see Arlock lying on the ground fast asleep!

I mean, was this where the poor man had been all along? Curled up on the rock-hard floor with his sleeping bag pulled right up under his chin? Certainly, he'd no idea he'd just been joined by a couple of desperate bat seekers.

'Wakey-wakey,' I whispered in Arlock's ear, only for him to cough and turn over, still fast asleep. Finn wasted no time shaking him so roughly that his eyes opened with a start.

'*Whas — whas* happening?' Arlock smiled weakly when he recognised us. But even I knew this was no time for pleasantries.

'We're looking for Shadow, that's what's happening. Where is he? Is he here with you?'

Arlock struggled upright. And I must admit, I struggled too, but in my case, it was to hide my shock. Even in the shadows of the cavern, it was obvious the poor man had aged twenty years since we'd last met. His skin was stretched tautly over his cheekbones, his eyes were ringed with dark circles, and his hands were shaking as they clutched tight hold of the sleeping bag. But even more upsetting was his mouth, which seemed to have sunk in on itself.

'What's all this nonsense about looking for Shadow?' Arlock wheezed, unable to hide his irritation. 'And why in heaven's name aren't you out there looking for The Dragondah Chronicles instead?'

Rather than answer, I reached out to feel his forehead.

'Are you okay, Arlock?' I asked gently, exchanging a worried glance with Finn. 'I mean, you don't *look* okay, you know. You're pale and you're clammy, and your breathing's not got any better, has it?'

But Arlock brushed me away, not just my hand but my concerns too. 'Oh, don't you fuss as well, Ottillee. I've already sent Vixen packing because her constant whining was driving me mad.' He tried to laugh, exposing even more of his pointed teeth. 'Now, how can I help you again?'

'You can help us by—'

'Getting yourself well,' Finn interrupted, throwing me a cautionary glance. 'Just tell us where Shadow is, and Ottillee and I will do the rest.'

But as was his habit, Arlock answered Finn's question with a question of his own.

'First, tell me *why* you need to find Shadow so urgently?'

'Because Shadow can save Dragondah Castle, that's why.'

'Yes, Shadow's our secret weapon, he is!'

'What in God's name are you talking about?' Arlock dragged himself to his feet with the help of the boulder. Now that he was no longer in the shadows, the bright light from the sunbeam only served to emphasise the harsh lines of his gaunt face. 'Shadow's some sort of secret weapon, you say? Have you both gone mad?'

'Of course not.' I quickly went over the astounding events of the last few days. That despite Arlock's well-meaning desire to protect us, we'd finally discovered who Lucifer Branson really was. That he'd actually been planning to kill Finn and had been a whisker away from killing Shadow too. I finished off by telling Arlock how our wonderful legal system always protected the underdog — or the under*bat* in this instance.

'Yes, you see it turns out that bats are a protected species here in the UK, and they'd already ruined Lucifer Crow's plans for one castle. So when he spotted Shadow flying about Dragondah Castle, the castle he *really* wanted, he thought the same thing was happening to him all over again!' I couldn't help grin at the memory. 'Honestly, Arlock, you should have seen the terrified look on Lucifer Crow's face when Shadow flew at him!'

He nodded thoughtfully. 'Mmmm, cowering on the ground like a cornered mouse, wasn't he?'

'Yeah, he's such a—' And then I fell silent. Something suddenly wasn't making any sense. 'But, Arlock, how do you *know* Lucifer Crow was cowering on the ground like a—? I mean, you weren't even there, were you?'

Arlock turned away, but not before wincing as though he'd said something he shouldn't.

'Yes, what a pity we didn't know bats had legal protection in this country,' he mumbled, almost to himself. 'If we had, things could have been different. Very different indeed.'

'Yes, but we know *now*,' I responded. 'And that's all that matters, doesn't it?'

I couldn't understand why Arlock wasn't — well, if not dancing a jig exactly, then at least *looking* a bit happier. After all, this was the breakthrough we'd been hoping for, wasn't it? We didn't need to find The Dragondah Chronicles to save the castle. We only needed to find Shadow.

'So come on, Arlock, where *is* my flittermouse?' This from an impatient Finn. 'He's not been home for days, and he wouldn't dare go to Dragondah Castle. So he *must* be here with you—'

'Sorry, lad, but it's no good.' Arlock rubbed a shaky hand over his face. 'You're too late.'

'What do you mean, we're too late?' I whispered.

'Shadow's gone.'

'*Gone?*' Finn grabbed Arlock's sleeve. 'You mean Lucifer Crow's trapped him again? Or Dagger—'

'No, no, it's got nothing to do with those two. It's just—'

'It's just *what?*'

'It's just that everyone has their time, lad, and Shadow — well, Shadow's had his.'

My heart began pounding in my chest. 'You're saying — you're saying Shadow's *dead?*' I breathed, hardly able to believe what I was hearing. Only six days ago, the bat had been zooming about the castle like he'd been putting on a show. Surely that hadn't been his last performance? But before I could say another word, Finn stepped forward, his face close to Arlock's.

'What did you do to him?' he snarled.

Arlock clung to the boulder, his expression desperate. 'I didn't do anything to him, lad.'

But Finn shook his head. 'I don't believe you, Arlock. I don't believe a single word you say. I knew you were bad news the moment I set eyes on you, and I was right. You've brought nothing but misery to Dragondah.'

'Oh, Finn, that's not fair,' I cried, but he took no notice.

'There's trouble everywhere you go, Arlock. And not just trouble but tragedy too.' Finn's eyes were glinting dangerously as they roved over Arlock's cowering frame. 'You and your mysterious warnings that always come too late. You let my parents die, you let my Shadow die, and you nearly let me die too. I HATE YOU!'

I gasped at the unconcealed hostility in Finn's eyes, as did Arlock.

'It was never my intention to hurt anyone, lad, believe me.'

But Finn just sank to the ground and covered his face with his hands. I tried to comfort him, but he was inconsolable, his bony shoulders heaving with sobs. Tears soon started filling my own eyes, not just because of Finn's anguish but also because I was never going to see Shadow again.

'Arlock, *please*,' I begged. 'Please help him.'

But he shook his head. 'I can't help him, Ottillee. I'm sorry, but we've reached the end.'

And now, this was the final straw for me too.

'Don't you *dare* give up, Arlock!' I cried, my eyes blazing. 'Now, I've had faith in you all along, haven't I? So, now it's time for you to have faith in me. This isn't the end. This is just the beginning — a brand new beginning for Dragondah and for all of us. So, will you *please* tell us what's happened to Shadow?'

Even now, Arlock refused to meet my gaze. 'Oh, Ottillee, you wouldn't believe me in a million years.' His eyes dropped to Finn, still huddled on the ground. 'Nobody would.'

'Look at me, Arlock,' I ordered as I took hold of his trembling hands. 'Finn's grieving for Shadow, that's all. He didn't mean what he said just now. Please remember we're on the same side here.'

Arlock looked even more anguished if that were possible.

'I know we are,' he whispered. 'But that's what makes everything so much worse.'

'But how?'

'Because Finn's right. I have let everyone down. I've let him down. I've let the Penhaligons down and—'

'Oh, please stop blaming yourself for every little thing.'

'And I've let you down too, Ottillee. I should never have

involved you in this mess in the first place. And now I've lost my shape — my *powers*, I mean, just when you and Finn need me the most.'

'No, we need *Shadow*, not you. Now come on, Arlock, for once in your life, tell us *exactly* what's going on. Please, I'm begging you.'

But Arlock shook his head as though regretting what little he *had* revealed. Honestly, what a nightmare we'd all suddenly found ourselves in. I didn't know whether to be angry with Arlock or feel sorry for him.

I mean, he'd lost everything, hadn't he? Shadow, Finn's parents, The Dragondah Chronicles, his health, and now his 'shape' and his 'powers', whatever the heck *they* were. Not only that, Arlock spent most of his time living in a cold, dark cave. And, to make matters worse, he'd got the world's scariest teeth. Especially now when they were more like *fangs—*

And then, all of a sudden, my body stiffened. My heart skipped a beat. My head filled with all sorts of strange thoughts and images. The cave. Vixen's sudden switch of loyalty. And what about losing Arlock right after that visit to Dragondah Peak? I'd never understood how *that* had happened. But no, surely I was wrong? That had to be impossible, didn't it? Suddenly the world as I knew it was shifting beneath my feet.

'You're Him, Aren't You?'

I STARED LONG and hard at the man slumped against the boulder in front of me. I was trying to recall a time when I'd seen Arlock and Shadow together. But I couldn't remember one single time. Arlock always seemed to vanish the moment Shadow showed up — and vice versa.

'Arlock, how come I've never actually seen you with Shadow?' I asked, keeping my voice calm. 'I mean, you talk about him a lot, but are you ever actually *with* him? No, not that I can remember.'

'Not now, Ottillee.' Arlock's voice was even quieter than mine.

'You're him, aren't you?' I whispered.

'Him?' Arlock treated me to a dull, blank look.

'Yes, *him*,' I repeated, hardly able to believe I was saying such a thing out loud. I mean, how on earth could Arlock the man also be Shadow the bat? Shapeshifting was nonsense, wasn't it? Something that only happened in films and fairy tales. But the more I thought about it, the more convinced I was. 'Yes, Arlock, you're Shadow, aren't you? You haven't lost your shape and your powers. You've lost your *shapeshifting* powers. That's what you meant, wasn't it?'

My gaze locked with Arlock's. Mine was steady. His was wavering. And now a heavy silence had descended over the cave, even Finn's sobs subsiding as he struggled to his feet.

'What the heck are you talking about, Ottillee? How on earth could Arlock be Shadow?'

I turned to Finn, taking in his flushed cheeks and his puffy eyes. How could I explain such an unbelievable thing to him when I was still struggling to explain it to myself?

'Oh, it's probably nothing,' I stalled, tossing Arlock a sideways glance.

'No, come on, Ottillee — tell me.'

Finn was refusing to be brushed off. Was this because he sensed I was on to something too? I took a deep breath and started talking.

'Well, okay, first, there's the teeth. Arlock and Shadow have both got, erm — the same teeth. And let's not forget they're both quite happy living in caves.' I couldn't bring myself to sneak another look at Arlock to see how he was taking this. 'Oh, yes, and the bad colds they both have — or *had*. How could I have missed that? It's the only thing that makes any sense.'

My conviction was growing stronger with my every word. I peeked at Arlock, only to see him looking — well, resigned, I suppose. But Finn was still full of questions.

'Well, it might make sense to you, Ottillee, but it makes no sense to me at all.'

'Then ask yourself this — have you ever seen Arlock and Shadow together?'

'Of course I have! Many times. At the — and then at the—' a puzzled Finn scratched his head. 'Although now I come to think about it, I don't suppose I have seen them together. Not in the same place at the same time, anyway.'

'That's exactly what I'm saying, Finn. Shadow only shows up after Arlock leaves. And the other way round. It happened when we first met Arlock, remember? Shadow flew into the cave clear as day. But when we followed him inside, who did we find in there?'

'Arlock.' Finn nodded slowly. 'And then when we left Dragondah Peek, we lost Arlock—'

'Only for Shadow to show up as though he'd never been away. Which he hadn't!' I was warming to my theme now. 'I mean, even *you* thought it was strange when Vixen went off with Arlock, remember? I mean, Vixen had always been your loyal friend up until then. And then, right out of the blue, she ups and leaves you for someone she's never even met before. Huh! I don't *think* so.'

'So you're saying Vixen already knew Arlock?'

'Of course she did. Vixen and Arlock have been friends forever. Or should I say Vixen and *Shadow?* Vixen's always known Shadow and Arlock are one and the same.' Suddenly I gasped. 'And don't you remember going on about how Arlock reminded you of somebody? Well, now you know who it was!'

'*What?* You're saying Arlock reminded me of Shadow?' Finn shook his head slowly. The blue-green eyes that met mine were strangely dull. 'But even I know best friends don't lie to you, Ottillee.'

'I'm not lying to you, Finn. I'm trying to help—'

'I'm not talking about *you*, Ottillee. I'm talking about Shadow! You're telling me he's not who I thought he was. You're telling me he's not a flittermouse, he's that—' Finn's eyes never left mine, 'he's that man over there!'

'He's a flittermouse *and* that man over there, that's what you have to understand!' I clutched hold of Finn's hand. 'I know it's difficult to believe in shapeshifters, but—'

'No, Ottillee, it's not difficult for *me* to believe in them.' Finn shook himself free. 'I told *you* about shapeshifters, remember, not the other way round. The only thing I'm struggling with is that I've been living a lie my whole life!'

Arlock stumbled forward now, his words coming out in short bursts. 'I never meant to deceive you, lad.' He reached out as if to pat Finn's shoulder before thinking better of it. 'It was for your own good, honestly it was. And I'm glad

the truth is out. I couldn't keep such a secret
from you forever.'

'Huh! I don't know why not!' A snarling Finn finally
turned to meet Arlock's gaze. 'You've been keeping it a
secret from me my whole life, haven't you? Sharing my
home, pretending to look out for me—'

'I *did* look out for you.'

'Oh yeah?'

'Yes, of course I did. That's what a Penhaligon wizard
does.'

'A Penhaligon *wizard?*' Finn and I chorused in wide-
eyed astonishment.

Although why we were so shocked, I don't know. If
Arlock had shapeshifting powers, then it was the only
thing that made any sense, wasn't it? I was just annoyed
it hadn't hit me before. With his odd habits and his
strange appearance, not to mention his uncanny ability to
know things he shouldn't, Arlock could hardly have been
anything *but* a wizard.

I glanced at Finn, who looked like he'd just been hit by
a ton of bricks. And then I glanced at Arlock who looked
like a ton of bricks had just been lifted off him. For the
first time in ages, he managed a genuine smile.

'Yes, just as Finn is the last in a long line of Penhaligon
kings, I'm the last in a long line of Penhaligon wizards,'
Arlock rasped, almost proudly now. 'I'm honoured to say

that for over one thousand years, it's been
my family's duty to look after the Cornish royal family.'

'How — when—?' I had so many questions I was fit to
burst. But even I knew they weren't mine to ask. I shot
another look at Finn, only to see his gaze fixed on the
ground as though he was trying to find the answers down
there. Again I realised it was up to me to try and make
sense of all this.

'But why did you protect Finn as a bat?' I asked. 'Why
didn't you protect him as the man you really are?'

'I had no choice, Ottillee.' Arlock's mouth twisted wryly.
'Nessa wouldn't let me have anything to do with Finn for
years. She blamed me for his parent's death, you see.'

'Why?' Finn's head shot up. His voice was as cold as ice,
but Arlock struggled on.

'Because I wasn't there when they died, lad. Cador was
my responsibility, you see. He'd always been a challenge,
of course.' A fond smile. 'Then one day, he begged to spend
a few days alone with your mum on the moors. Some sort
of second honeymoon, I believe. They were forced to
shelter beneath a tree during a storm, and that flash of
lightning — well, it came out of nowhere apparently, and
they never stood a chance.'

Finn and I gasped. No doubt he was picturing the same horrific scene as me. Two lives snuffed out in seconds, a baby boy waiting for them back home. Unsurprisingly, I was the first to recover.

'But the lightning strike wasn't *your* fault, Arlock. I mean, it was just a tragic accident, wasn't it?'

'Tell that to Nessa, child. And to my conscience too. All I can say is that I've been trying to atone for the deaths of Cador and Rebecca Penhaligon ever since that fateful day.' Arlock's sunken eyes turned in Finn's direction now. 'By protecting the life and the legacy of their orphan son.'

I glanced at Finn, nervously waiting for his reaction. It was a while coming.

'Nan's speaking to you now though, isn't she?' was all he managed to get out, his voice flat with no trace of emotion.

'Oh, yes, Nessa and I have developed what you might call a love-hate relationship, lad.' Arlock allowed himself a smile, clearly relieved Finn was prepared to *listen* to him at least. 'Actually, Nessa *had* to talk to me if she wanted to protect your inheritance. I'd realised something was up when I spotted a Crow snooping about your castle back in the spring.'

'Is that when you told Nanna Nessa who you were?'

'Yes, indeed, lad.' Another wry smile. 'I thought it was about time.'

'So you confessed you'd been sleeping in the corner of

our home for the past ten years, did you?' A bitter twist of Finn's mouth now. 'I'm sure that went down well.'

'Oh, Nessa was shocked to the core at first, but she's lived in Dragondah a long time. She knows we live by different rules here.' Arlock looked at Finn from under his brows. 'And it's not like she's unfamiliar with shapeshifters, is it?'

'Yeah, hard to believe, isn't it?' Finn shook his head ruefully. 'Nan scares me to death with an imaginary shapeshifting dragon when all the while she's got a *real* shapeshifting bat — sorry, wizard living in her own home.'

'The irony wasn't lost on Nessa either, lad, believe me. But she accepted my deception had been for the right reasons. And as soon as she heard that one of the Crows was sniffing about this place again, she also accepted it was time for me to tell you who you were. No matter you were still quite a few years off sixteen yet.'

Arlock took some deep breaths and steadied himself against the boulder.

'Do you need to rest a minute?' I asked him gently.

'Oh, Ottillee,' Arlock smiled fondly at me. 'Cowenna couldn't have chosen anyone better to take over Dragondah Hall. We'd never have got anywhere without you.'

'*Really?*'

'Yes, of course. Nessa knew Finn wouldn't take kindly to a stranger like me turning his life upside down.'

'That's not fair!' cried Finn.

'Isn't it, lad? You hardly welcomed me with open arms, did you? No, Nessa knew you'd need support from someone your own age. Someone who'd once lived in the real world. Someone who hadn't been wrapped in cotton wool their entire lives.' Arlock ignored Finn's frustrated curse and smiled at me instead. 'And if that *someone* happened to have been chosen by Cowenna Penhaligon, then all the better. Nessa and I would wait patiently for this unknown Ottillee Bottomly girl to get here. And then I'd introduce myself to her as soon as possible—'

'Introduce yourself?' Something suddenly hit me. 'Oh, my gosh, Arlock! You — I mean *Shadow* — flew over my house that first day on purpose, didn't you?'

'Of course I did, Ottillee! Without you, our mission would have been doomed before it had even begun.' To my horror, Arlock suddenly crumpled to the ground. 'Not that it isn't doomed anyway.'

'But the mission *isn't* doomed,' I insisted as I knelt down next to him. 'Shadow can save it.'

'No, he can't, Ottillee.'

'Arlock, you don't understand.' Now it was Finn's turn to offer assistance, and he reached down to cover the wizard's frail body with his sleeping bag. 'The quicker you turn back into Shadow, the quicker we can get the castle back.'

'No, lad, it's *you* who doesn't understand.' Arlock clutched tight hold of Finn's hand. 'I'd do anything to help you, lad, honestly I would. Since the day you were born, Vixen and I have saved you from falls, drowning, and even toadstool poisoning on one particularly scary occasion. Truth is, we've saved you from all manner of dangers.'

'Then *please*, Arlock, please bring my Shadow back.' Finn's expression was desperate. 'One last time even. Just for me to say goodbye to him.'

'But that's just it, Finn, I can't.' Arlock squeezed his eyes shut as though he was in pain.

'But why *not?*' Finn cried, and I threw him a cautionary look. Arlock was struggling now, every word taking its toll on him.

'Because shapeshifting's a gift, Finn. One of the greatest gifts a wizard is ever given. But like all gifts, it has a habit of running out.'

'What do you mean?'

'Every time I shapeshift, I become weaker, lad. I lose a part of myself, a part of the man I really am. Especially if I do it too often and don't give myself enough time to recover.'

'You mean Arlock grows weaker as Shadow grows stronger,' I whispered as a recent image of the bat soaring about the castle filled my mind. And now, here was Arlock, slumped on the ground as if he only had hours left to live.

'Yes, Ottillee, my heart will fail if I don't use all my powers to regain my strength.' Arlock's body was suddenly racked with coughs. 'Shadow's slowly taking me over. And

I know that if I turn back into him one more time before I'm ready, I'll never be able to turn back into Arlock. I'll be Shadow forever.'

A heavy silence fell. Second after second, the only sound in the cavern was Arlock's laboured breathing. Then suddenly, Finn put his face right next to the wizard's.

'So, do it, Arlock.'

'What?'

'Change back to Shadow one more time.'

'Finn, no!' I cried, terrified by such an order.

But Finn kept his eyes on Arlock. 'He needs to do his duty to my family, Ottillee. He needs to save the castle—'

'But didn't you hear what he just said?'

'I heard everything he said, Ottillee. I certainly heard him say he'd do anything to help me.'

'But you'll *kill* him, Finn! His heart will fail him!'

'I don't care, Ottillee. Arlock failed me *and* he failed my dad, so I won't miss him for one single day of my life.' Finn's voice faltered. 'But I'll miss Shadow for every single second of my life.'

Arlock met Finn's gaze for a long moment.

'The lad's right, Ottillee. I've got to give it one more go. And as this may well be the last time I speak to you—'

'No!'

'—I must insist that you never tell another living soul what you've learnt about me today. It's a Penhaligon secret of the very highest level.' When Finn nodded in agreement, Arlock struggled upright. 'Now, just give me some privacy, will you? I need to get myself under that beam of light over there and—'

'No! No, I won't let you!' I turned to Finn, my eyes wide with desperation. 'Don't ask him to do this, Finn, or you'll never forgive yourself.'

'But I'm the last Penhaligon, Ottillee.' Finn seemed filled with some strong, almost overpowering emotion. 'I'll never forgive myself if I destroy King Locryn's legacy.'

'And I'll never forgive you if you destroy another human being.' I grabbed his hand. 'A human being who's devoted his whole life to you, Finn.'

Our eyes locked for a few heart-stopping seconds. Tears suddenly began rolling down Finn's cheeks.

'Forgive me, forgive me, Ottillee,' he whispered over and over again. 'I don't know what I was thinking.'

And then he crumpled to the ground.

———◦◦◇◦◦———

33

Dad's Secret Report

DATE: Friday, 24 August, 2018   TIME: Middle of the night

PLACE: Bedroom, of course   SUBJECT: Where do I start?

Dear Dad,

I feel terrible. I've got so many things wrong...

1) Arlock's not who I thought he was. But I can't tell a single soul because he swore me to <u>absolute</u> secrecy. Not that Mum would ever believe he was a shapeshifting wizard anyway. I mean, would you? And now the poor man's disappeared again. I only hope he's not fighting for his life all alone somewhere. (Surely Vixen's gone with him, wherever he is?) Even worse, Finn and Nanna Nessa have taken off without a word too. There's just a dead patch of grass and a wonky old water tap where their horsebox used to be. But I <u>know</u> I was right to insist that Arlock's life was more important than getting Dragondah Castle back.

2) And talking of the castle, Mum's old friend Lucifer is even <u>more</u> of a phoney than I thought he was. Yes, he's lied his head off about EVERYTHING, including his last name. (He's really Judas Crow's son!!!!?) And he's still lying his head off today. According to yesterday's Cornish Clarion, he's 'devastated' (what a joke!) that some recent health and safety issues have forced him to pull out of the children's academy. But so as not to let the council down, he's now decided to turn Dragondah Castle into the new HQ for his global charity empire. Global <u>smuggling</u> empire, more like. In fact, now I come to think about it, this was Lucifer's plan all along. To follow in his father's footsteps. I mean, you've got to hand it to the old scavenger, haven't you? He's a clever one.

3) Much cleverer than me, anyway. Because I hate to admit it, Dad, but I've finally run out of ideas for saving Dragondah Castle. There's nowhere left to look for The Chronicles. Shadow can't come to our rescue anymore. And I simply can't fight Lucifer Crow all by myself. Especially as he was right — I mean, this isn't really <u>my</u> fight, is it? I <u>am</u> just a blow-in with no links to either the Penhaligons <u>or</u> Dragondah. I just wish that you were still here, Dad. Mum's doing her best to be supportive, but group hugs don't really work with two people, do they?

Lots and lots of love,
Your mergh,
Ottillee xoxoxo

PS: My eczema's suddenly flared up again. And I've got a <u>really</u> sore throat. Let's hope I'm not coming down with something because I'm supposed to be starting school in ten days. But if you <u>don't</u> hear from me for a while, it'll probably be because I'm too weak to lift a pen.

34

'I'm Fine, Mum, Honestly I Am.'

'NOW, OTTILLEE, are you quite sure you've had enough to eat?' Mum was backing out of my attic bedroom, a tray in her hand and a sympathetic expression on her face. 'Or could you manage another slice of cake?'

'No, I'm fine, Mum, honestly I am.'

I'd been in bed for five days now, suffering from what the doctor called 'bronchitis', but what Mum called 'stress, low spirits, and the inevitable result of racing through damp caves without a thermal vest.'

There was no doubt I hadn't been at all well, my temperature and breathing only just back to normal. I was eating better now too, certainly Mum's banana cake if not her spinach soup. But I knew I had to get my strength back if there was any chance of me starting at my new school on Tuesday.

And I was really hoping I *would* be strong enough because it was doing me no good at all lazing about in bed tormenting myself over every single thing that had happened these past few months, *years* even. Dad's death. My strange legacy. Arlock's shapeshifting. Finn's disappearance. The upsetting discovery that Mrs Crow had used me for revenge. And now my own dismal failure at preventing Dragondah Castle from being taken over by Lucifer Crow.

I picked up *Cornwall's Fascinating Flora and Fauna*, to take my mind off things, but the book simply wasn't fascinating enough for me. Not the chapter on 'Sessile Oaks', not the one on 'Grey Seals', not the one on 'Areas of Outstanding Natural Beauty', and especially not the one on 'Sphagnum Moss'. Although I'd decided that was the perfect name for the speckled raven that was still taking a great interest in all the comings and goings at Dragondah Hall.

And then suddenly, I heard the familiar sound of Lucifer Crow's helicopter flying overhead, and I slammed the book down on my bed. Because it wouldn't be long before *this* 'Area of Outstanding Natural Beauty' was again poisoned by the villainous activities of his family. Smuggling and murder ran through their veins, just as this magical if thoroughly exasperating corner of Cornwall now ran through mine.

I lay back against my pillows and gazed fondly about my sunlit room. Nowadays, I found myself taking great comfort in the age of things. The waxy sheen on the antique chest. The scratches in the wooden floorboards. And the way the timber rafters and beams might look a bit rough and ready, but would still be here for centuries to come.

Yes, my modern London posters were starting to look really out of place in my cosy little rooftop eerie, particularly the shocking pink 'Keep Calm, I'm a Girl Guide' one. Perhaps it was time to rip it down and replace it with something more appropriate? *Meaningful* even. Maybe I could frame one of Mum's paintings when she'd actually finished one? Or even Arlock's old map of Dragondah as a reminder of what Finn and I had tried so hard to achieve this past month?

Mind made up, I got out of bed, padded over to the poster and ripped it off my wall with the same determination I ripped a plaster off my knee. And then my knees almost buckled with shock. Because there were some words carved into the timber post behind it. And they read...

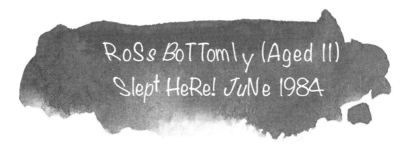

Ross Bottomly (Aged 11)
Slept Here! June 1984

My eyes were riveted. My mind was racing. I mean, surely this was some kind of cruel joke? Surely my dad hadn't slept in this very attic when he was the same age as me? And then, as I prodded the rough lettering with my fingertips, I got an even bigger shock. The timber post swung out of the wall to reveal — well, what it revealed I'd no idea. I hardly dared breathe. I hardly dared look. But when I *did* summon up the courage to peer inside, it was to see a hiding place containing a single envelope. A single envelope addressed to me. Picking it up with trembling fingers, I ripped it open and started reading the letter inside...

FROM THE DESK OF COWENNA CROW
DRAGONDAH HALL ● CORNWALL

My dearest Ottillee,

What a relief — you found my letter, just as I hoped! Please excuse the games of a dying old lady, but I simply had to leave its discovery to destiny. After 100 years of living on this earth, I've learnt to trust destiny far more than people, I'm afraid.

I'm now about to reveal the truth about you, your family and your new home here in Dragondah. I'll admit I had every intention of letting these secrets die with me, but your poor father's shocking death forced me to reconsider my legacy.

I loved Ross Bottomly very much, you see. Not for the bogus reasons I led you to believe, but because he was my great-nephew. Yes, there's a surprise for you, Ottillee. Ross stayed with me here several times as a boy. I like to think it was his secret weekends at Dragondah Hall that fuelled not only his passion for nature but also his adventurous spirit — believe me, if your father wasn't seal-spotting in Dragondah Bay or bird-watching on Dragondah Island, he was chasing dragonflies round my beautiful garden! And let's not forget how he carved his name on one of the posts in his beloved attic 'den'. Yes, Ross was thrilled when he stumbled upon my secret hiding place. And even more thrilled when he discovered the 'treasure chest' I'd stowed away in there.

Ross was brought to Dragondah Hall by his grandmother Lucy who sadly died long before you were born. Lucy was my beloved older sister and the only member of my family to have anything to do with me after my ill-fated marriage to Judas Crow. Lucy's continued devotion was all the more remarkable as by this time, she'd made a new life for herself in London as the wife of Arthur Bottomly. And what a lovely man your great-grandfather sounded like, I must say!

But now I will get to the purpose of my letter, Ottillee. Which is to tell you that you are a member of an extraordinary family, a nugget of information your father was never privy to. You see, both your great-grandmother Lucy and I were born Penhaligons, a royal dynasty that once ruled Cornwall from their castle here in Dragondah. And as the direct descendent of two Penhaligon princesses, Dragondah Castle and everything that goes with it, could now be yours. Yes, that's right, child! And all you need to do to prove your legacy is to find that 'treasure chest' your father held so briefly in his 11-year-old hands.

I really did my best to keep *The Dragondah Chronicles* away from what I call 'prying eyes', first in Dragondah Hall's library, and then in your attic bedroom. But about ten years ago, my rather arrogant great-nephew Cador Penhaligon turned up on my doorstep and insisted on moving them 'back where they've always belonged'.

He was furious that Lucy had entrusted them to me just before the last war when the whole world was in turmoil. Only the heir to the Cornish throne should know where *The Chronicles* are hidden, he'd insisted with his usual high-handedness. But I've long had eyes for spying and ears for eavesdropping, haven't I? After all, my own brother Jago Penhaligon was once the heir to the throne himself. So, I've no doubt where Cador buried *The Dragondah Chronicles*, and that's beneath King Locryn's secret tomb on Brimstone Moor. Yes, Ottillee, Brimstone Moor, the location of your new school.

I truly believe that if you're anywhere near as spirited as your father Ross you'll have no trouble finding The Dragondah Chronicles. And that if you're anywhere near as caring as your great-grandmother Lucy, the future of both Dragondah Castle and Dragondah Hall lies in very good hands.

Much love from your Great-Great Aunt Cowenna,

PS: Cador died shortly after taking The Chronicles. I should warn you that his orphan son also has a strong claim to the castle. (You'll probably see your cousin scrumping apples from the garden.) The boy himself won't discover his royal heritage until he's 16, although no doubt he's already as high and mighty as his father and grandfather before him! So, I think it's finally time for another branch of King Locryn's family to step into the spotlight, don't you? I'm just so sorry I never met you, Ottillee.

I stumbled backwards towards my bed.

Oh, my gosh! Oh, my gosh! Oh, my gosh!

I was a member of Cornwall's long-lost royal family.

I myself.

Me.

Ottillee Bottomly!

But far more important than that, I was Finn's cousin!

I hadn't just got myself a wonderful new house here in Cornwall, but I'd got myself a wonderful new family too. Amazingly, Mrs Crow hadn't left me Dragondah Hall out of revenge, but out of love for my *dad*. I mean, what better reason could there be?

And as I lay back down on the bed, my tearful eyes skimmed my great-great aunt's letter over and over again. Her legacy had given me so much more than I could ever have dreamed possible. And now I'd been given the push I needed to return the favour. Not only to justify the old lady's faith in me but also to honour Dad's memory.

I just wished Mrs Crow had swallowed her bitterness and got to know Finn better. Because if she *had* knocked on the window when he was scrumping her apples, she'd have discovered her great-great nephew wasn't high and mighty at all. Was in fact, caring and clever and courageous and the perfect person to lead Dragondah out of the darkness and into the light. With me right beside him, of course.

'Mum!' I yelled from the top of the stairs. 'I've got something to tell you!'

———◇◇◇◇———

FIRST MYSTERY SOLVED!

Thank you so much for reading Part One of

The Dragondah Mysteries. From a strange legacy to

a missing fortune, only 11-year-old Ottillee Bottomly

has the courage, conviction (and nerve!) to solve them all.

Her adventures with Finn continue, of course, and you just

have to turn the page to get an idea of what happens next...

Jackie Loxham

xox

  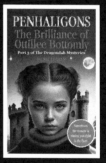

THE DRAGONDAH MYSTERIES

DRAGONDAH • BRIMSTONES • PENHALIGONS

From Amazon and select bookstores

www.jackie-loxham.com

BRIMSTONES

Ottillee's Adventures Continue...

'*OTTILLEE BOTTOMLY!*'

'*Yes, Mrs Grail?*'

'*I won't tell you again. If you don't sit still, close your eyes, and clear your mind of all your fears and worries,*' the headmistress's voice hardened suddenly, '*I'm going to come over there and make you.*'

'*Ooops, yes, sorry, Mrs Grail.*'

I ignored the twins (Abby and Gabby did everything together, even snigger) and tore my gaze away from the windows. Problem was, I could control my body, but I couldn't control my mind. Because somewhere on the other side of those diamond-shaped panes of glass, beyond the manicured lawns, past the shimmering lake, amidst the gorse-covered moorland, maybe even at the top of that distant and rather hazy purple hill, was King Locryn's secret tomb. Oh yes, and *The Dragondah Chronicles*.

So, how could I be expected to 'clear my mind of all my fears and worries' when the fate of Cornwall's long-lost royal family was resting on my very own shoulders? And when a criminal mastermind was about to turn my favourite place in the world into a haven for bullies, imposters, smugglers, bat killers, child snatchers and possibly even worse. Not that Mrs Grail knew this, of course. No, she assumed I was like the rest of my classmates after the first week at our new school. That all my 'little problems' could be solved by one of her stress-busting yoga classes.

And I have to admit, Brimstone High School for Young Ladies was the sort of place where stress needed busting. It certainly lived up to its claim as 'the oldest learning establishment in the British Isles' anyway. And I wasn't just talking about its maze of medieval buildings with their draughty walkways and their lofty pillars and their stained glass windows. Or the fact that there were so many cherubs, crosses and candelabras about the place that I hardly liked to talk above a whisper.

No, it was the old-fashioned (and possibly criminal) way of life here. I mean, hadn't chalk and algebra and lacrosse and Latin and liver and semolina already been banned in British schools? And if they hadn't, then it's about time they were.

As for the school's 'off-the-beaten-track moorland setting', all that had done was encourage quite a few of the teachers to go off the beaten track themselves. Take Mrs Grail herself, for example. One minute the headmistress was leading morning assembly in a flowing black gown with her hair in a bun like any normal woman round about my mum's age. The next minute she was shaking out her long brown curls, squeezing herself into purple lycra and forcing us all into the Lotus position....

A NOTE FROM THE AUTHOR

Please give a rating or leave a review!

I really hope you've enjoyed reading about Ottillee's adventures in Cornwall. Your opinion truly matters to me so it would mean the world if you'd take a minute to leave a review or rating on Amazon or with your local bookstore. (If you're under 13, please ask a grown-up to do this for you.) A sentence or a click is often all it takes to introduce more parents and children to The Dragondah Mysteries. Your kind feedback is very much appreciated and so important to me. Thanks so much for your time!

——⚬⚬✕⚬⚬——

Keep in Touch!

And if you'd like to keep in touch, just go to www.jackie-loxham.com. I'd really love to hear from you, and you can also take a peek into Ottillee's world!

Jackie Loxham

xox

Printed in Great Britain
by Amazon